Ripley's Believe It or Not!®

Developed and produced by Ripley Publishing Ltd

This edition published and distributed by:

Mason Crest
450 Parkway Drive, Suite D, Broomall, PA 19008
www.masoncrest.com

Copyright © 2010 by Ripley Entertainment Inc. This edition printed in 2013.
All rights reserved. Ripley's, Believe It or Not!, and Ripley's Believe It or Not! are registered trademarks of Ripley Entertainment Inc. No part of this publication may be reproduced in whole or in part, or stored in a retrieval system, or transmitted in any form or by any means, electronic, mechanical, photocopying, recording, or otherwise, without written permission from the publishers. For information regarding permission, write to VP Intellectual Property, Ripley Entertainment Inc., Suite 188, 7576 Kingspointe Parkway, Orlando, Florida, 32819
website: ripleybooks.com

Printed and bound in the United States of America

First printing
9 8 7 6 5 4 3 2 1

Ripley's Believe It or Not!
Beyond Reason
ISBN: 978-1-4222-2774-9 (hardback)
ISBN: 978-1-4222-2791-6 (paperback)
ISBN: 978-1-4222-9035-4 (e-book)
Ripley's Believe It or Not!—Complete 8 Title Series
ISBN: 978-1-4222-2769-5

Cataloging-in-Publication Data on file with the Library of Congress

PUBLISHER'S NOTE
While every effort has been made to verify the accuracy of the entries in this book, the Publisher's cannot be held responsible for any errors contained in the work. They would be glad to receive any information from readers.

WARNING
Some of the stunts and activities in this book are undertaken by experts and should not be attempted by anyone without adequate training and supervision.

BEYOND REASON

www.MasonCrest.com

BEYOND REASON

Unbelievable stories. Read about mind-boggling tales and intriguing incidents. Meet the man with over 200 national flags tattooed on his body, the 15-in (38-cm) hairball found inside a girl's stomach, and a fridge that is shaped like a coffin.

This 19th-century circus sideshow performer was covered in lots of wooly hair…

Ripley's Believe It or Not! | BEYOND REASON

RAISE THE FLAGS

Guinness Rishi from Delhi, India, was featured in *Ripley's Believe It or Not! Seeing is Believing* for a stomach-churning ketchup-guzzling feat. Now Guinness has undertaken to get his head, face, and body permanently tattooed with more than 200 national flags in full color. Guinness has 24 flag tattoos on the top of his head, 25 flags on his face, and more than 150 other flags on the rest of his body. He is now working on tattooing a map of the countries of the world on his stomach.

TATTOOS SO FAR!

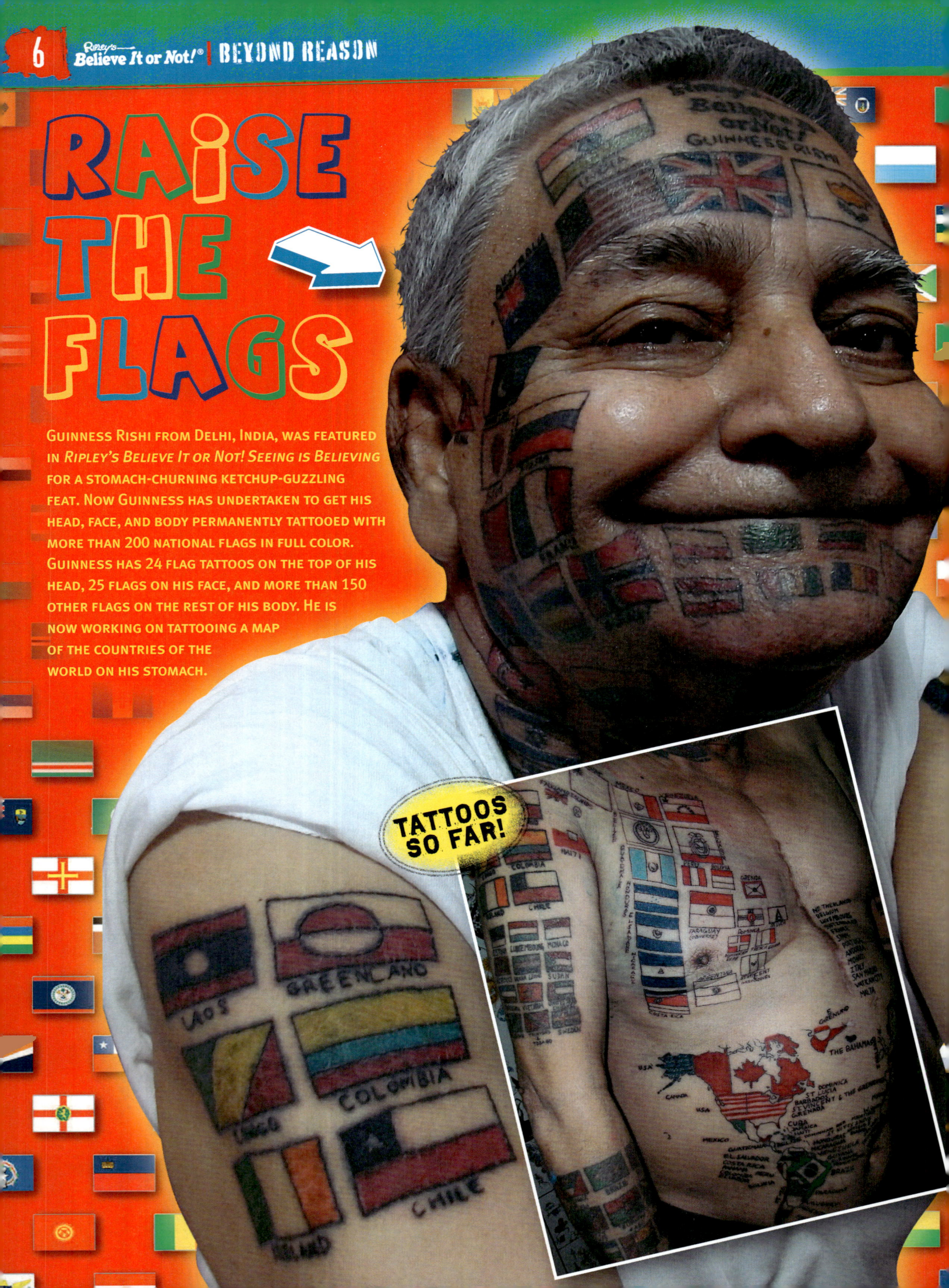

CLEVER GIRL
Born in 2006, Karina Oakley of Surrey, England, had an IQ of 160 at just two years old—the same as eminent scientist Stephen Hawking and Microsoft chairman Bill Gates. Karina, whose IQ is 60 points above the British average, was asked to complete a 45-minute test in several different categories, including verbal ability, memory, numbers, and shapes.

PADDED BRA
Brazilian Ivonete Pereira's life was saved in April 2009 when a robber's bullet struck a wad of cash hidden in her bra. The 58-year-old had stuffed the bills in her bra because robbery was rife in her local area.

FAT REMOVAL
A half-ton teenager from Houston, Texas, had 70 lb (32 kg) of fat cut off in an operation. Billy Robbins, who at his heaviest weighed 840 lb (380 kg), underwent the radical procedure to prevent his heart from giving out.

NEEDLE REMOVED
Doctors in China removed a syringe needle from 55-year-old Lao Du 31 years after another doctor broke it off in his butt cheek.

SPEARGUN
In March 2009, Emerson de Oliveira Abreu of Brazil accidentally shot himself in the head with a speargun. Despite it going 6 in (15 cm) into his skull, he survived.

FACE TRANSPLANT
Surgeons replaced 80 percent of the face of Connie Culp from Unionport, Ohio, in a 2008 operation, using the bone, muscles, nerves, skin, and blood vessels of another person. It was the world's most extensive face transplant surgery ever.

BLOOD LOSS
Named after a French neurologist, "Cotard delusion" is a rare mental disorder in which a person believes he or she is either dead, does not exist, is putrefying, or has somehow mislaid his or her blood and internal organs.

WHEELY ODD
Many-times world beard champion Elmar Weisser of Baden, Germany, has styled his long beard into designs of Berlin's Brandenburg Gate, London's Tower Bridge, and, in 2009, a bicycle. It takes up to five hours to style his beard for each competition.

BIG APPETITE
A former basketball player-turned-street-performer, Zhao Liang, from China's Henan province, stands nearly 8 ft 1 in (2.45 m) tall—and feeds his enormous appetite with a dinner of eight burger-sized steamed buns and three plates of food.

GLASS CHIN
While shaving in 2009, Thomas Entwistle from Bolton, Greater Manchester, England, discovered a piece of glass from a Ford Cortina windshield embedded in his chin 30 years after the accident that put it there.

HAIR-RAISING
A bullet fired at the head of Briana Bonds of Kansas City, Missouri, in February 2009 was caught in her tightly woven hair weave. The wig saved her life and she escaped unharmed.

BEARD DAY
To mark the 200th anniversary of the birth of evolutionary biologist Charles Darwin, who was born on February 12, 1809, England's Bristol Zoo allowed free admission on February 12, 2009, to anyone sporting a beard—real or fake.

Sheep Man
"Rham Sam" was a circus sideshow performer in Europe in the 19th century whose body exhibited a mass of sheeplike wooly hair. He is shown here in London in 1890 with lecturer Professor Langdon.

Ripley's Believe It or Not! BEYOND REASON

DREAM MACHINE

A Brooklyn-based artist collaborative—Ghost of a Dream (Lauren Was and Adam Eckstrom)—created a life-size replica of a Hummer H-3 from $39,000-worth of losing lottery tickets. Their artwork, titled "Easy Money, Dream Car," features windshield wipers, tires, and body panels made entirely from lottery tickets. The wheel hubs are plastic casts of coin-covered hubcaps to represent the tool people generally use to scratch off the tickets.

MASS ASCENT
In 2009, a total of 326 hot-air balloons took to the skies simultaneously at the Lorraine Mondial Air Balloons rally in eastern France.

TRUCK SHOWER
A Chinese truck driver was fined in 2009 for having a shower while driving along the country's busy Jinyi expressway. Police officers stopped the truck after spotting water leaking from the cab, but were shocked to see that the driver was soaking wet and had been enjoying a shower from a sprinkler system installed above his head. His wife, sitting in the passenger seat, had been holding up a sheet of plastic to protect the vehicle's instruments from the water.

MAIL BOAT
The mail boat *J.W. Westcott II*, based in Detroit, Michigan, delivers mail to other vessels that pass along the Detroit River and even has its own postal zip code, 48222.

MINI MOTOR
Perry Watkins from Buckinghamshire, England, has created a roadworthy car that is only 39 in (1 m) high and 26 in (66 cm) wide. Remembering the children's TV character, Watkins bought a Postman Pat coin-in-the-slot children's ride on the Internet, reinforced its fiberglass shell with a steel frame, and mounted it onto a mini four-wheeled bike before adding a 150cc engine, mirrors, windshield wipers, and lights.

CROC WALK
A 12-in-long (30-cm) baby crocodile caused panic among passengers on an EgyptAir flight from Abu Dhabi to Cairo in July 2009 when it decided to take a walk down the aisle of the airplane.

SCHOOL RUN
Having missed his bus one morning in January 2009, a six-year-old boy from Richmond, Virginia, took the keys to his family's Ford Taurus car and decided he would drive to school. He crashed into a utility pole on the way, but escaped with only minor injuries.

ECO TRAVELERS
Eco-friendly Tom Fewins and Lara Lockwood of Oxfordshire, England, traveled more than 44,000 mi (70,800 km) around the world in 297 days—without once boarding an airplane. They made their way through 19 countries—including Russia, China, and the United States, using 78 buses, 61 trains, 34 cars, 18 boats, 6 bicycles, 2 mopeds, and 1 elephant. They say they each generated less than 6,600 lb (3,000 kg) of carbon dioxide on their journey, one-third of the amount they would have generated if they had traveled by airplane.

CARDBOARD CARS
Police in Sibiu County, Romania, use cardboard cutouts of patrol cars on roadsides to frighten speeders into slowing down.

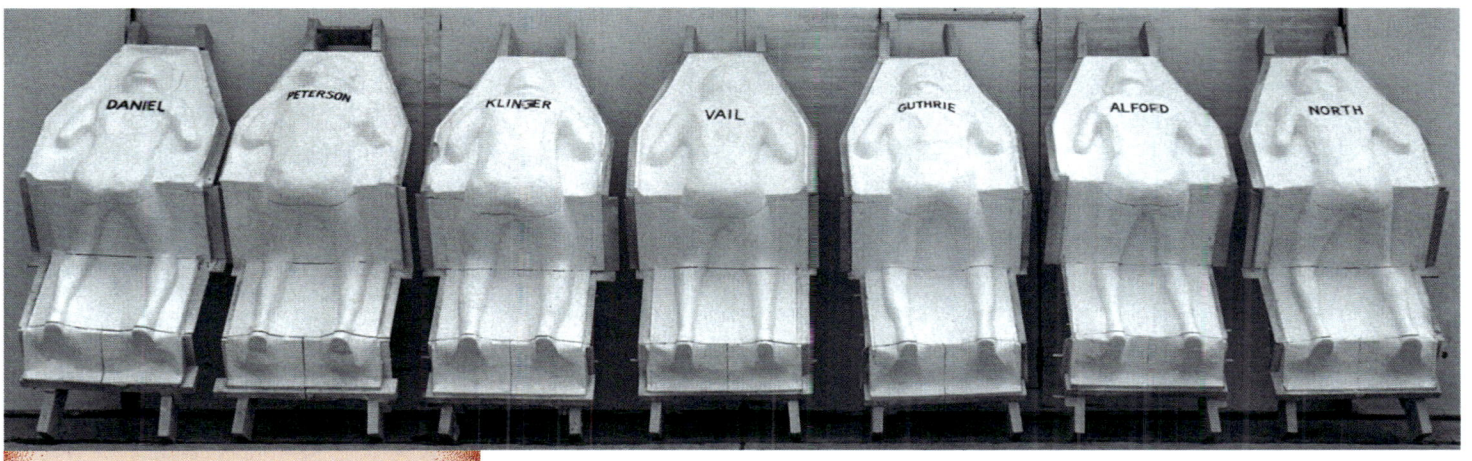

Butt Molds

In the early days of NASA, for reasons of comfort and safety, astronauts on manned space missions sat on couches individually molded to fit their body shape. None of the names on these test seats—pictured at NASA's Langley Research Center at Hampton, Virginia, in 1959—made it aboard the pioneering *Mercury* spacecraft: they belonged to NASA employees.

R STUDENT PRANK

Pranksters from the Massachusetts Institute of Technology in Cambridge placed a 25-ft-long (7.6-m) fire truck on top of the school's Great Dome building in 2006. The joke followed a noble tradition. A fiberglass steer from a local restaurant was placed on the dome in 1979, as was a phone booth in 1982, and in 2003 a 45-ft (14-m) replica of the Wright brothers' biplane mysteriously appeared on top of the Great Dome to mark the 100th anniversary of flight.

R ROMANTIC ROAD

When it was constructed in 2003, the M6 motorway toll road near Birmingham, England, was paved with 2.5 million pulped Mills-and-Boon romantic novels. The books' paper helps keep the road's tarmac in place and also absorbs noise.

R AUDI PARTNER

An Audi car that an elderly woman from Hildesheim, Germany, reported stolen resurfaced two years later buried beneath a layer of dust in her neighbor's garage. She had asked mechanics repairing the car in 2007 to return it to her garage, but they had mistakenly put it in her neighbor's unused garage, where it had remained undetected until the summer of 2009.

R HOMEMADE HELICOPTER

Despite having only a basic school education, 20-year-old Wu Zhongyuan of Luoyang, Henan Province, China, in 2009, made his own helicopter, which he claims can fly to a height of 2,625 ft (800 m). It took him nearly three months to build his flying machine, which has a motorcycle engine and wooden blades made from an elm tree.

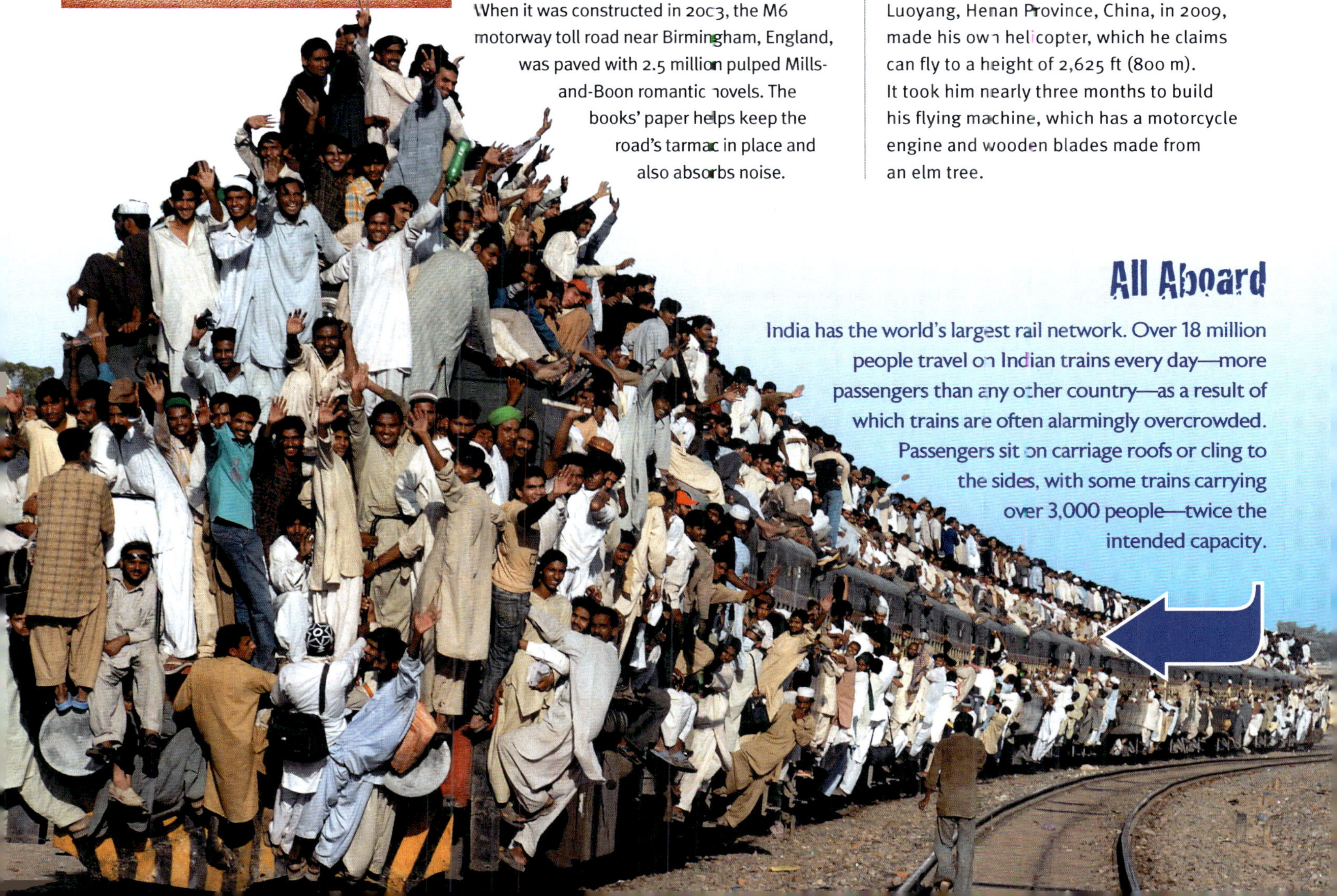

All Aboard

India has the world's largest rail network. Over 18 million people travel on Indian trains every day—more passengers than any other country—as a result of which trains are often alarmingly overcrowded. Passengers sit on carriage roofs or cling to the sides, with some trains carrying over 3,000 people—twice the intended capacity.

BEYOND REASON

Goodbye Rocco by Jorge Perruorria is a 1950s fridge made to look like a brightly colored coffin.

Fridge-tastic

An unusual art exhibition in Paris, France, entitled "Energy-Devouring Monsters" featured more than 50 refrigerators. Transformed into colorful works of art by Cuban artists Mario Miguel Gonzalez (known as Mayito) and Roberto Fabelo, the fridges are all classic 1950s models, which were commonplace in Cuban homes until the country replaced all high-energy consuming appliances during an energy crisis in the 1990s. These fridges were saved from the scrapheap and now enjoy a new lease on life in this unique display of icons from Cuba's past.

Fast Food by Luis Enrique Camejo marries a fridge with the front of a 1950s American car in a comment on the consumerism of that era.

ENORMOUS ECLAIR
In February 2009, the Swallow Bakery of Chichester, West Sussex in England, made a chocolate eclair that was nearly 12 ft (3.6 m) long. The monster eclair contained 2.2 lb (1 kg) of chocolate and 8 pt (3.8 l) of double cream. It took bakers Lou Allen and Michaela Heard four hours to construct the pastry, followed by another hour filling it with cream before spreading the chocolate on top.

TASTY ORGANS
A restaurant in Tokyo, Japan, serves up sushi body parts hidden inside an edible human "corpse." The corpse, which has a dough "skin" and "blood" sauce, is wheeled into the restaurant on a hospital gurney and placed on a table. The hostess begins by cutting into the "body" with a scalpel, after which the patrons also dig in, opening up the flesh to reveal edible "organs" made of sushi.

HIDDEN ENTRANCE
Evening visitors to The Safe House restaurant in Milwaukee, Wisconsin, are asked for a password to gain admission to the spy-themed eatery and bar, which has a hidden entrance and a secret exit.

PANCAKE BLAST
With their pancake-in-a-can product, workers from the Batter Blaster company made an amazing 76,382 pancakes in eight hours at Atlanta, Georgia, in May 2009. The team used more than 30 grills on the challenge.

OLIVE THEFT
One morning in May 2008, olive grower Quentin von Essen from the Hunter Valley, New South Wales, Australia, woke to discover that all but two of his 400 olive trees had been stripped overnight by thieves. Apart from the two untouched trees, which were spotlit, the thieves did not leave a single olive on any tree or on the ground—and some of the trees were 11 ft 6 in (3.5 m) tall.

PIZZA LINE
In May 2009, Scott Van Duzer and nine other cooks prepared more than 1,800 pizzas to form a pizza line measuring 1,777 ft (540 m) around an entire city block in Fort Pierce, Florida. It took 1,250 lb (570 kg) of flour, 600 lb (270 kg) of mozzarella cheese, 70 gallons (265 l) of tomato sauce, and 400 tables to form the line.

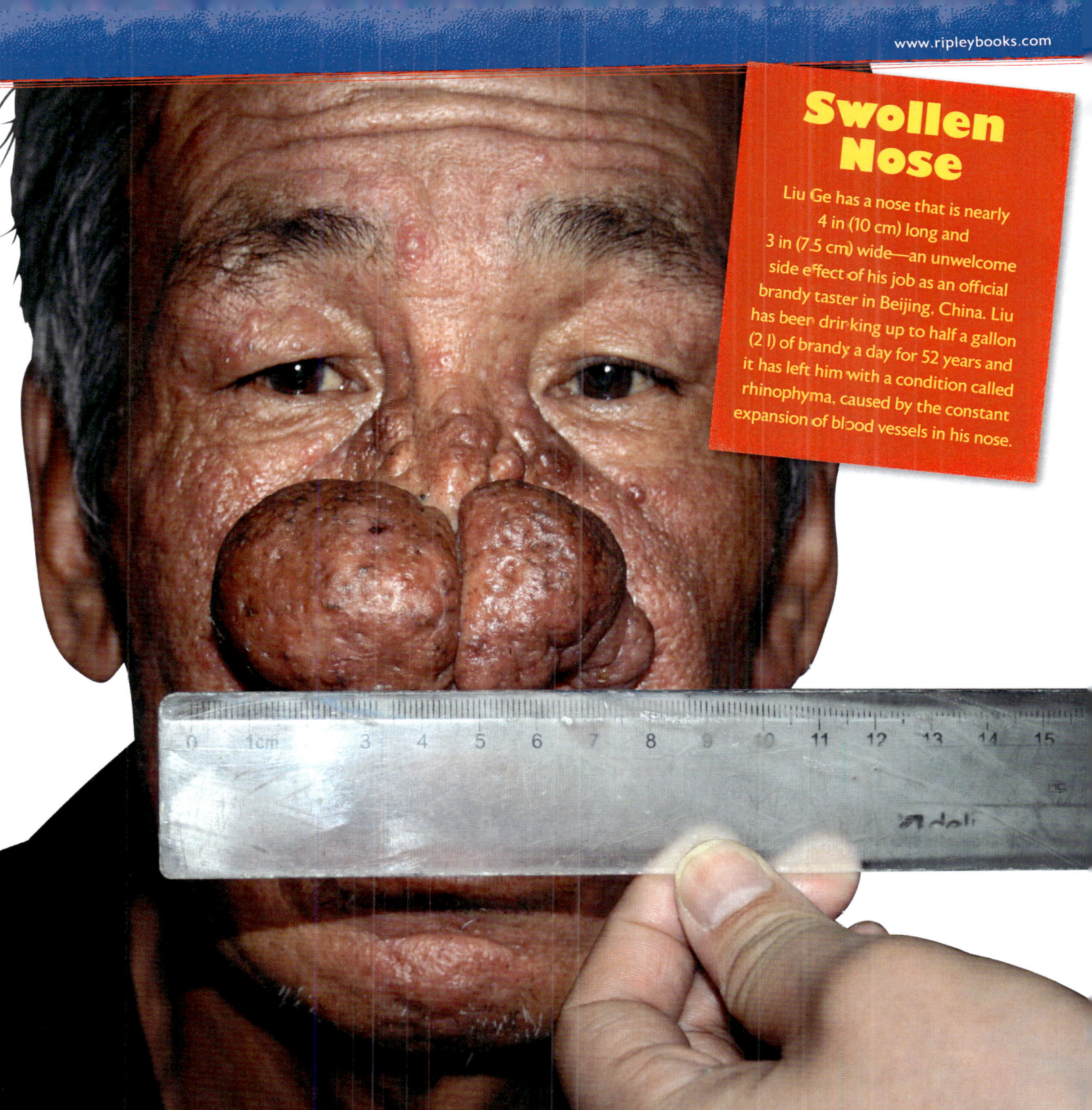

Swollen Nose

Liu Ge has a nose that is nearly 4 in (10 cm) long and 3 in (7.5 cm) wide—an unwelcome side effect of his job as an official brandy taster in Beijing, China. Liu has been drinking up to half a gallon (2 l) of brandy a day for 52 years and it has left him with a condition called rhinophyma, caused by the constant expansion of blood vessels in his nose.

R LOBSTER ROLL
Using 48 lb (22 kg) of lobster meat and 4 gal (15 l) of Miracle Whip, the people of Portland, Maine, in June 2009 baked a lobster roll that measured 61 ft 9½ in (18.8 m) long.

R COLD COMFORT
Immigration officials in Llandudno, Wales, found a Chinese chef living in a freezer inside a restaurant where he was employed.

R PURPLE PEARL
A Florida couple stumbled across a potential fortune in their seafood dinner. George and Leslie Brock were eating steamed clams at a restaurant in Lake Worth when Mr. Brock bit on something hard—a rare, perfectly round purple pearl. Purple pearls are most commonly found in large New England quahogs—clams known for violet coloring on the inside of their shells— and the finest specimens can be worth as much as $25,000.

R STURDY TOASTER
Joan Lopes of Suffolk, England, regularly uses an electric pop-up toaster that is nearly 60 years old. She bought the silver toaster as a wedding anniversary gift for her parents in 1951.

R PIZZA DELIVERY
In November 2004, Lucy Clough from Sussex, England, hand-delivered a pizza from London to Melbourne, Australia— a journey of 30 hours and a distance of 10,532 mi (16,950 km).

BEYOND REASON

Tasty Treats

From smoked rattlesnake to creamed armadillo, there is some crazy canned food available around the world for those with adventurous taste buds. Try popular foods, such as cheeseburgers, or more gruesome offerings, such as the silkworm pupae (left) or ants' eggs, there is something to suit everyone—you can even buy a whole chicken in a can, complete with bones and skin!

® MANY BEERS
Over 5,000 different types of beer are brewed in Germany. There are about 1,300 breweries in the country, and the Weihenstephan Abbey Brewery in Bavaria has been making beer for nearly a thousand years—since 1040.

® ROTTEN STENCH
In May 2009, rotten food in a refrigerator released odors so vile that hundreds of people were evacuated from a building in San José, California, and seven others were sent to the hospital. One of the few people who didn't need treatment was the office worker who was cleaning out the fridge at the time—suffering from allergies, luckily she couldn't smell a thing.

® POISON ROOT
Cassava root, a common tropical food source, contains cyanide and can poison a person if it is not prepared correctly.

® GLOWING JELLO
By including food-safe quinine as an ingredient, gastronomes Sam Bompas and Harry Parr from London, England, have created a jello that glows blue in the dark.

® MARS CROP
NASA scientists say that the soil on Mars would be good enough to grow asparagus and turnips, but unfortunately not fertile enough for strawberries.

® CHICKEN FEED
The average meat-eater consumes 1,200 chickens per person during his or her lifetime—that's 3,970 lb (1,800 kg) of chicken meat, the equivalent of eating a four-year-old elephant.

® SUPER SANDWICH
In June 2009, the Bradley County Chamber of Commerce made a 168-ft-long (51-m) BLT (bacon, lettuce, and tomato) sandwich at the 53rd Annual Bradley County Pink Tomato Festival in Warren, Arkansas. The sandwich, which took nearly two hours to build, used 300 lb (136 kg) of bacon, 80 lb (36 kg) of lettuce and 60 lb (27 kg) of tomatoes, and oozed 220 fl oz (6.5 l) of mayonnaise.

® ROMANTIC CHEESE
In the 12th century, Blanche of Navarre tried to win the heart of French King Philippe Auguste by sending him 200 cheeses every year.

® COSTLY CURRY
To coincide with the DVD release of Oscar-winning movie *Slumdog Millionaire* in June 2009, Bombay Brasserie restaurant in London, England, prepared a curry that cost $3,000 a portion. The dish, called the Samundari Khazana, or Seafood Treasure, contained Devon crab, white truffle, Beluga caviar, quails' eggs, sea snails, and a Scottish lobster coated in edible gold leaf.

® SNAKE BITE
Until health authorities stepped in to stop the practice in 2009, a prized delicacy on the menus of restaurants in the southern Chinese province of Guangdong was meat from a chicken that had been bitten to death by a poisonous snake.

® GARLIC BALLS
American First Lady Eleanor Roosevelt used to eat three chocolate-covered garlic balls every morning. They were prescribed by her doctor to improve her memory.

® LETTUCE EUPHORIA
Lettuce has the same effect on rabbits as opium has on humans. Lettuce contains lactucarium, which has been used as a sedative in sleeping draughts and can cause a sense of mild euphoria in rabbits.

® CRAZY CRAVINGS
Thirty-seven-year-old Rakesh "Cobra" Narayan, of Moala, Fiji, will eat just about anything—including floor tiles, pieces of concrete, clothes, shoes, furniture, and even a lawn mower. His crazy cravings started when he was ten and chewed some chicken wire. Then, because he was still feeling hungry, he ate a raw chicken. Now he eats nuts and bolts, insects, lizards, grass, grease, and his favorite, broken fluorescent-tube lights. At first the sharp objects used to cut the inside of his cheeks but since he learned to cope with the diverse materials in his mouth, he claims to have never suffered any ill effects.

® INSECT DIET
A mountain hiker survived five days after a bad fall on a mountain by eating centipedes, ants, and even a poisonous wolf spider. Derek Mamoyac from Philomath, Oregon, was descending 12,300-ft (3,750-m) Mount Adams in Washington State in October 2008 when he fell and broke his ankle. Despite his injury, he continued his descent by crawling or, if that became too painful, shuffling on his backside. When his food supplies ran out, he ate insects to keep his strength up.

SNAKE WOMAN

In 2009, surgeons in China removed a tumor from a woman's leg that weighed three times more than she does. The non-cancerous growth started out as a birthmark on the body of Wang Houju from Linxi, Shandong Province, but steadily wrapped itself around her leg and up to her waist, earning her the name of "Snake Woman." Eventually, it weighed over 220 lb (100 kg), whereas the rest of her body tipped the scales at just 70 lb (32 kg).

RAW TALENT

Jia Jem decided to make this stylish dress out of raw meats when she had nothing to wear to a friend's party. Jia, from Chicago, Illinois, made the dress out of salami because it's thin and stays in one piece, and bacon because it looks meaty. She started with a basic thick cotton dress, layered the meat on top then covered it with a clear vinyl. The dress took her six hours to make and was refrigerated until it was time for the party.

GENETIC MIRACLE

In a genetic phenomenon that is at least a one in 500,000 chance, a British couple have given birth to their second set of twins where one daughter is white and the other black. In 2001, when Dean Durrant and Alison Spooner from Hampshire, England, were told they were having twins, they were stunned to discover that one daughter, Lauren, took after her mother with blue eyes and red hair, while her sister Hayleigh resembled her father who is of West Indian origin. Then, in 2008, history repeated itself when Leah was born white like her mother and her twin sister, Miya, had her father's darker skin.

DEXTROUS FEET

Forty-nine-year-old Jana Blazova of Presov, Slovakia, learned to use her feet to write and embroider despite being paralyzed by cerebral palsy in childhood.

DELAYED DEATH

Fifty-four-year-old Craig Buford of Fort Worth, Texas, died on December 29, 2008, from complications of a gunshot wound he had sustained 35 years earlier.

Soft as a Peach

Using 24,000 peaches, this sculpture of Australian actress Jolene Anderson was made and displayed in Sydney's First Fleet Park, Australia, in 2008. An advertising agency constructed the 39-ft (12-m) model to promote a skincare range. With the key slogan "Skin good enough to eat," the work was intended to remind Australian women that their skin is soft and fragile, like a peach. What a shame the peaches will eventually rot!

Ripley's Believe It or Not! | BEYOND REASON

Freed Frog
In 2007, an eight-legged frog was saved from the cooking pot at a restaurant in Quanzhou, southeast China. The one-of-a-kind frog was close to contributing its legs to one of the restaurant's famous frogs' legs dishes, but compassionate staff decided to keep the animal instead of cooking it!

R CALAMARI KING
Patrick Bertoletti of Chicago, Illinois, ate 6 lb 10 oz (3 kg) of deep-fried calamari in ten minutes at Mallie's Sports Grill World Calamari Eating Championship, held in Southgate, Michigan, in May 2009.

R POLICE BALL
A 267-lb (120-kg) matzo ball was unveiled on the streets of New York City in August 2009. Baked by Noah's Ark Original Deli, it was 3 ft (1 m) high and made from 1,000 eggs, 80 lb (36 kg) of margarine, 200 lb (90 kg) of matzo meal, and 20 lb (9 kg) of chicken base. The ball was transported in a 24-ft (7-m) freightliner with a police escort.

R TURKEY TREAT
A farm in Devon, England, created a roast dinner consisting of a huge turkey stuffed with 11 smaller birds—a goose, a chicken, a pheasant, and eight young ducks. Weighing 56 lb (25 kg), the True Love Roast was big enough to feed 125 people.

R POTATO DIET
Joanne Adams from Cleveland, England, used to live on 16 bags of potato chips a day. For some 20 years she ate hardly anything but potatoes, and as a result she kept breaking fingers and her hair grew so slowly she needed to wear extensions.

DUCKLING DELICACY

DUCKLING EMBRYOS THAT ARE ALMOST READY TO HATCH ARE A CULINARY TREAT IN THE PHILIPPINES. KNOWN AS BALUT, THE POPULAR DELICACY IS SOLD BY STREET VENDORS ACROSS THE COUNTRY. GETTING THE BALUT EGGS TO THIS STAGE IS A PAINSTAKING PROCESS, AS THEY HAVE TO BE CAREFULLY INCUBATED FOR 17 TO 20 DAYS—UNTIL THE DUCKLINGS ARE ALMOST READY TO HATCH—BEFORE THEY ARE PART-BOILED AND SOLD. BALUT HAS BECOME SO POPULAR YOU CAN EVEN GET BOTTLED BALUT, PICKLED BALUT, AND BALUT OMELET.

PECKING POINTERS
Balut etiquette

- Balut should be eaten in a certain way to get the most from the egg's contents.
- First, tap the shell to make an opening large enough to get the fetus broth, or soup.
- Drink this soup, which tastes light and quite sweet, through the hole before peeling the shell to reveal the yolk and pre-developed duckling.
- Everything inside the egg can be eaten, although most people add some salt and pepper or chili to the fetus before chewing!

CREAM TEA
In May 2009, Anne Tattersall from Devon, England, created an enormous cream tea, featuring a scone that weighed 99 lb (45 kg) and measured 3 ft (1 m) in diameter. The scone was baked by Nick, Amy, and Mary Lovering and Simon Clarke and was filled with 20 lb (9 kg) of jelly and 35 lb (16 kg) of clotted cream.

TASTY JAIL
Inmates at Parappana Agrahara prison in Bangalore, India, refused to apply for bail because the jail food was so good. Juvenile offenders even lied about their age to get in. It may be no coincidence that the prison recently housed 4,700 inmates—more than twice its capacity.

CHOWDER CROWD
At the 28th annual Chowderfest held in Boston, Massachusetts, in July 2009, 2,000 gal (7,570 l) of New England's signature dish of clams, cream, and potatoes were served to a crowd of around 10,000 people.

FISH MADNESS
Some herbivorous fish can cause a form of food poisoning that can bring on severe hallucinations when eaten.

MOVING HEART
When April Pinkard's doctor examined her to treat a rare medical condition, he couldn't find her heartbeat—because her heart had moved to the other side of her chest, occupying an empty space where a damaged lung had once been. Her heart kept floating around her body until April from Live Oak, Florida, was finally given breast implants to keep it in place.

BILLION FROGS
Up to one billion frogs are eaten by people around the world each year.

WORM CANDY
Annie Munoz of Panama City, Panama, makes candies filled with grasshoppers and mealworms, and lollipops with worms inside. She hopes to sell them to the rest of Central America and China.

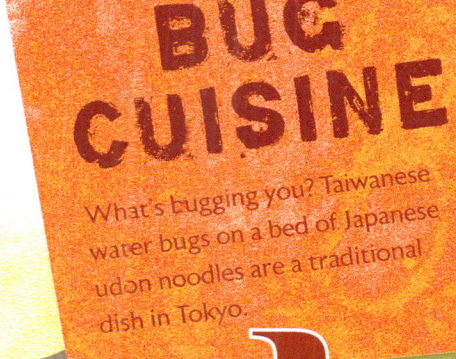

BUG CUISINE

What's bugging you? Taiwanese water bugs on a bed of Japanese udon noodles are a traditional dish in Tokyo.

BEYOND REASON

R RUDENESS PAYS
A bar in the Spanish resort of Cullera offered free beer and tapas in 2009 to customers who insulted its bartenders. The owners of Caso Pocho said the gimmick was designed to relieve stress among its recession-weary clientele, but added that the free alcohol and snacks would go only to those who came up with truly original insults.

R HOSPITAL FOOD
Hospitalis, a restaurant in Riga, Latvia, is hospital-themed with waitresses dressed as nurses, food served in flasks, cocktails served in test tubes and beakers, and medical implements for cutlery.

R EGG-STREME DIET
To build up their body weight for the 2010 Commonwealth Games, India's rugby players were ordered to eat seven meals and at least 15 eggs a day for over a year.

R PIZZA RUSH
Dennis Tran of Silver Springs, Maryland, made three large pizzas in just over 46 seconds in 2008—that's an average of around 15 seconds per pizza. He had to hand-stretch the fresh dough, apply pizza sauce, and top the three pizzas—one pepperoni, one mushroom, and one cheese.

R SAUSAGE SUPPER
In 2009, cooks from Vinkovci, Croatia, used a vast 8-ft (2.5-m) pan to prepare a sausage that was 1,740 ft (530 m) long and fed around 3,000 people. The sausage was made with 880 lb (400 kg) of pork (from 28 pigs), 88 lb (40 kg) of paprika, 22 lb (10 kg) of salt, 11 lb (5 kg) of garlic, and 5 lb 8 oz (2.5 kg) of spices.

R PANCAKE STACK
Sean McGinlay and Natalie King of the Hilton Grosvenor Hotel, Glasgow, Scotland, took 22 hours to build a pancake stack that stood 29½ in (75 cm) high. The tower of 672 pancakes used 100 eggs, more than 17 pt (8 l) of milk, 11 lb (5 kg) of flour, and 6½ lb (3 kg) of butter.

R SPACE PEE
The International Space Station has a $250-million water regeneration system that changes urine into drinkable water.

R RICH CAKE
In July 2009, 170 Palestinian bakers from ten pastry shops in Nablus on the West Bank created a giant syrupy Kunafa cheesecake that measured 243 ft (74 m) long, weighed 3,883 lb (1,765 kg), and was big enough to feed more than 100,000 people. The bakers used 1,540 lb (700 kg) of semolina flour, the same amount of cheese, and 660 lb (300 kg) of sugar to make the cake at a cost of about $15,000.

R CHILI GRENADES
To control rioters and fight insurgents, Indian security forces have been conducting trials using hand grenades that contain red-hot chili powder. The grenades use Bhut Jolokia chilis, which are 200 times hotter than the average jalapeno, to choke rioters' respiratory tracts and cause their eyes to water.

R LONG SERVICE
At age 95, Angelo Cammarata retired following over 75 years as a bartender at his family's café in Pittsburgh, Pennsylvania. He served his first drink as a 19-year-old just minutes after Prohibition ended in 1933 and, except for a 30-month break during World War II, he tended the bar right up until 2009.

Mice Kebab
After being killed in the fields of Malawi, mice are boiled, dried, salted, and sold by children as lunch to passing travelers. For easy handling, half a dozen of the sun-dried rodent carcasses are inserted in a piece of split bamboo. The heads are left on, so the customer eats everything—including the mouse's hair, bones, teeth, tail, and toenails.

RED HOT

Brave contestants devour red hot chili peppers in a speed-eating competition in Guizhou, China. Chili peppers are measured in Scoville Heat Units (SHU), which relate to the number of times a chili extract must be diluted in water to lose its heat. The naga morich chili pepper from Bangladesh measures a tongue-numbing 1,500,000 SHU, making it no less than 50 times hotter than cayenne pepper.

BEYOND REASON

CHARMED LIFE
Ninety-year-old grandfather Alec Alder from Gloucestershire, England, reckons he has cheated death no fewer than 14 times. He has survived several car crashes, a 15-ft (4.5-m) fall from a tree as a boy, war-time bombing, being run over by a tank, and he even walked away after a fighter jet smashed into the side of his house as he slept. Perhaps his narrowest escape came in 1939 when his wedding prevented him from being sent to Dunkirk, where his whole army squadron was killed.

PIGEON FANCIER
Former U.S. boxing champion Mike Tyson once booked a hotel suite in Louisville, Kentucky, for his eight favorite pigeons.

DOUBLE VISION
A set of identical twin brothers married a pair of twin sisters in a military ceremony in Pechora, Russia, in 2009. Lilia and Liana Kobozevsa were indistinguishable in their matching white dresses, while the only slight difference between Alexei and Dmitry Semyonova was the shade of their dark suits.

SHREK WEDDING
Living up to his name, Keith Green married Christine England in Devon, England, in April 2009 dressed up as the movie character Shrek. He and his bride —who was dressed as the ogre Princess Fiona, also from the movie *Shrek*—spent three hours having their faces and hands painted green.

DIVIDED HOUSE
A couple in Cambodia who separated in 2008 after nearly 40 years of marriage decided to divide their belongings equally— by taking the unusual step of sawing their house in half. The wife stayed in the remaining upright half of the house while her husband carried away his half to a field on the other side of the village where he planned to start a new life.

PRIZED MUSTACHE
Many police departments throughout India offer bonuses and prizes for officers that grow mustaches.

Hairy Meal
An 18-year-old girl was so addicted to eating her own hair that a massive hairball measuring 15 x 7 in (38 x 18 cm) formed in her stomach. The teen had complained to doctors of abdominal pains and vomiting and that's when they discovered the 10-lb (4.5-kg) mass of dark, curly hair, which filled almost her entire stomach.

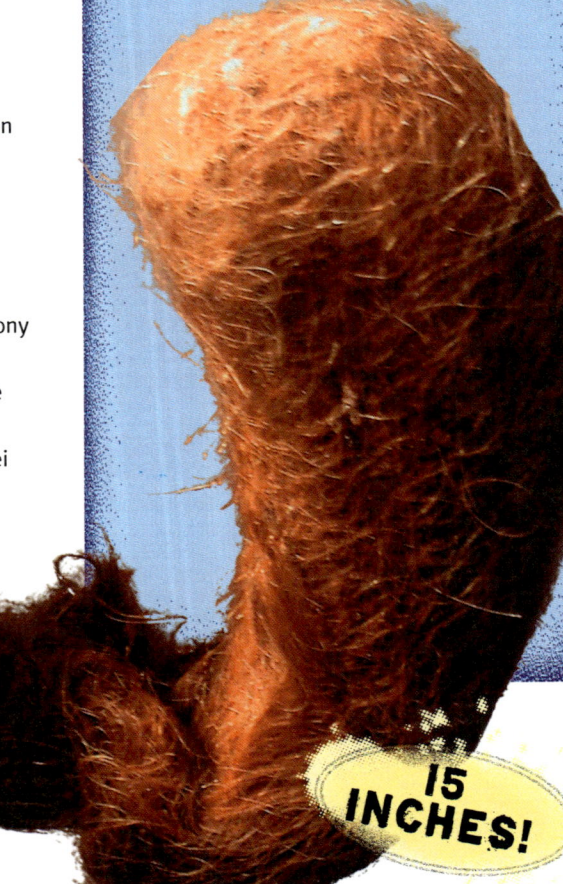

15 INCHES!

COMPUTER CASKET
The family of a computer geek have stored his remains inside an old PC. The computer displays a plastic plaque bearing his name, Alan, and the dates of his birth and death. Friends were encouraged to pay their tributes by writing messages on Post-it notes and slipping them through the floppy drive slot.

SPACE ODDITY
Canadian circus tycoon Guy Laliberté was blasted into space as a space tourist in 2009, dressed as a clown. The founder of the Cirque du Soleil wore a bulbous red clown nose and took along more red noses for his crew mates on the International Space Station.

FEIGNED DEATH
A 22-year-old Japanese man feigned death for three hours in a failed attempt to avoid being arrested for driving into a police motorcycle. After fleeing the scene of the accident, he collapsed and pretended to be dead even after a catheter was inserted into his urethra by paramedics.

KEEPING ACTIVE
Xie Long from Chongqing, China, kept fit for 30 years using two old mortars as dumbbells— until a friend noticed the weapons were still live. Police defused the mortars, which could have exploded at any time.

TRAIN ORDEAL
An American tourist survived for 2½ hours clinging to the outside of a train as it sped through the Australian outback at up to 70 mph (110 km/h). Chad Vance from Alaska jumped on to The Ghan, which travels from Adelaide to Darwin, as it was pulling out of a station in June 2009. As the express train gathered speed, he squeezed himself into a precarious stairwell until a crew member finally heard his cries for help and brought the train to a halt.

ALCOHOLIC SOAP
A hand gel intended to combat swine flu was withdrawn from use at a British prison in 2009 after inmates realized it contained alcohol and starting eating it. Instead of rubbing the liquid soap on their hands, inmates at Verne Prison, Dorset, England, put their mouths over the dispensers and started consuming significant quantities of the gel, with the result that a number became involved in a drunken brawl.

KNUCKLE CRACKER
Donald L. Unger of Thousand Oaks, California, cracked the knuckles of his left hand—but never his right—every day for more than 60 years to investigate whether frequent knuckle cracking could lead to arthritis of the fingers.

BACK FROM THE DEAD
Found lying in a pool of blood from a head wound at her apartment in Cernavoda, Romania, 84-year-old Elena Albu was declared dead by a doctor. However, when a forensic photographer took her picture, she opened her eyes and complained of a headache.

Giant Hand

Liu Hua from Jiangsu, China, had an operation to remove 11 lb (5 kg) of tissue from the index finger, middle finger, and thumb of his left hand. Before the operation his thumb measured 10½ in (26 cm) long, his index finger was 12 in (30 cm), and his middle finger 6 in (15 cm)—and his thumb and index finger were thicker than his arms! The total weight of his left arm was a whopping 22 lb (10 kg).

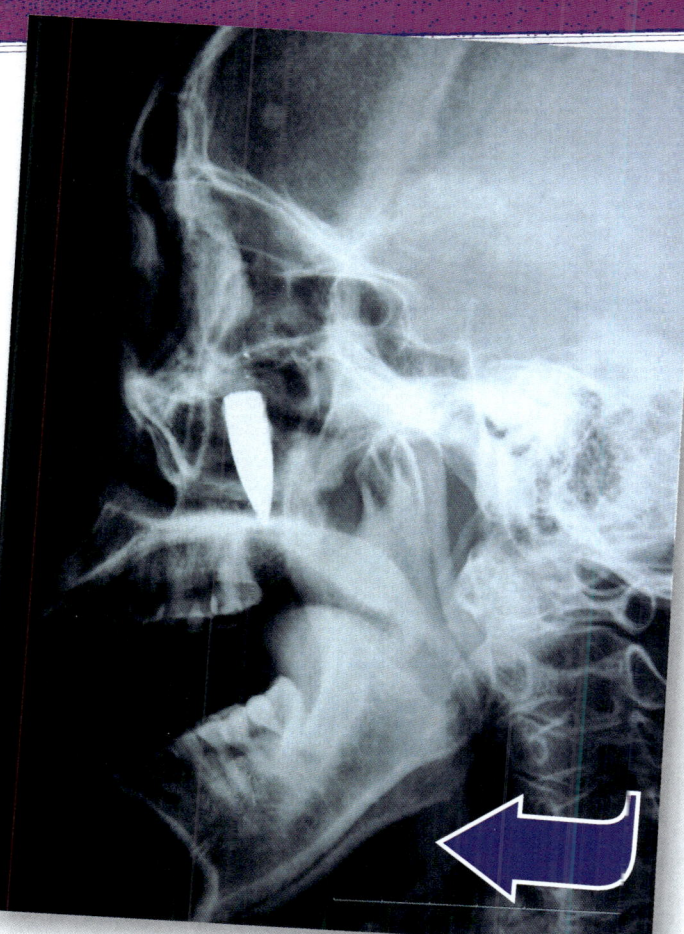

Bullet Pain

A bullet 1⅓ in (3.3 cm) long that had been lodged in a Chinese woman's face for 42 years was finally removed after she complained of blinding headaches. Hou Guoying had been mystified by the presence of the bullet until she remembered being accidentally shot with a starting pistol during the 1967 Cultural Revolution.

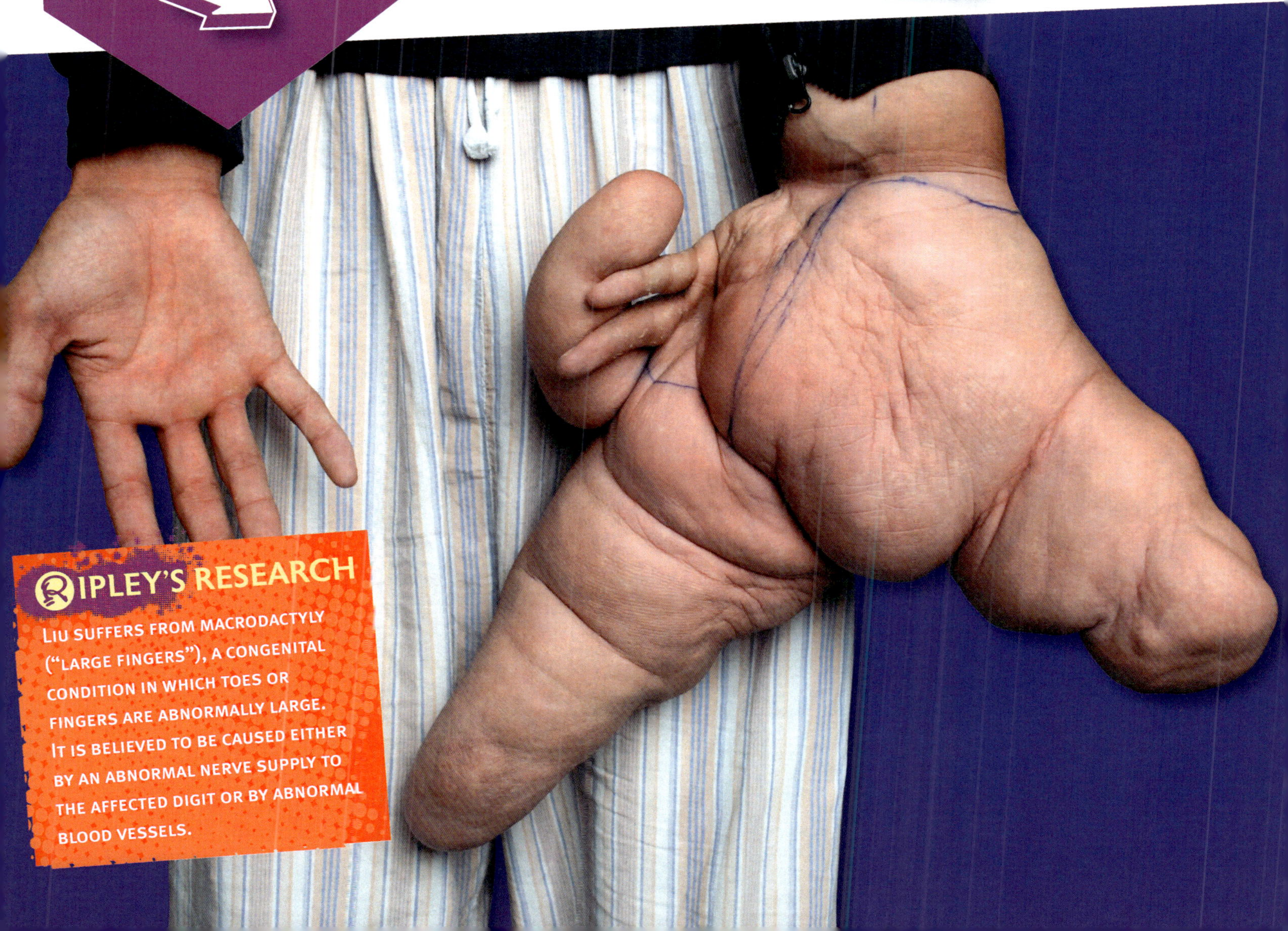

Ripley's Research

Liu suffers from macrodactyly ("large fingers"), a congenital condition in which toes or fingers are abnormally large. It is believed to be caused either by an abnormal nerve supply to the affected digit or by abnormal blood vessels.

BEYOND REASON

R GRATE DRAIN ROBBERY
Between 2007 and 2008, thieves stole more than 2,500 manhole covers and storm drain grates from the streets of Philadelphia, Pennsylvania, to sell as scrap metal.

R HOSPITAL CRECHE
The state of Nebraska has a law that allows a person to leave a child of any age at a hospital without risk of prosecution for abandonment. One of the first parents to use it dropped off nine children aged one to 17!

R $500,000 DOG
A woman in China paid over $500,000 for a Tibetan mastiff dog in 2009. Mrs. Wang had spent years scouring China for the perfect specimen, a dog called Yangtze River Number Two. When the pet arrived by plane at Xi'an airport, it was met by banners, a welcoming committee of local dog-lovers, and a motorcade of 30 luxury limousines sent by the new owner's wealthy friends.

PERSONAL URNS

Cremation Solutions of Arlington, Vermont, offers a unique memento of the dearly departed—an urn shaped like their head. A full-sized head, created from photographs of the deceased and able to hold the ashes of any adult, costs $2,600, and the company can even add a wig to the urn if the customer wishes.

Wily Coyote
A coyote struck by a car at 75 mph (120 km/h) near the border of Nevada and Utah was found embedded in the front fender eight hours later—still alive! The coyote not only survived the impact and the 600-mi (965-km) journey, it was even well enough to escape from its rescuers.

FIVE WEDDINGS
Simone and Ryan Feeney from Buckinghamshire, England, got married five times in less than a year. They first tied the knot in March 2008 at the Little White Wedding Chapel in Las Vegas, Nevada, and followed it up over the next ten months with ceremonies in Turkey, Britain, the United States (again), and Australia.

SCREAMING CONTEST
Russian Sergey Savelyev can scream at 116.8 decibels—that's about as loud as an ambulance siren. He demonstrated his shrieking ability when picking up $900 for winning an international screaming contest in Pattaya, Thailand, in August 2009.

SILENCE IN COURT!
Annoyed by repeated interruptions in court, a judge ordered the defendant's mouth be taped shut. Judge Stephen Belden, of Canton Municipal Court in Ohio, decided that putting duct tape over the mouth of robbery suspect Harry Brown was the only way to restore order.

WEDDING TOAST
Opening their presents following their wedding at Howden Minster, East Yorkshire, England, in 2009, Claire and Stuart Linley were amazed to discover that they had been given no fewer than 24 toasters. They kept one and returned the other 23.

BOG CHAMPION
Bride-to-be Casey Squibb of Dorset, England, went bogsnorkeling on her bachelorette party—and ended up recording the fastest time ever for a woman at the Irish Bogsnorkeling Championships in Castleblayney, Monaghan. She took 22 friends to Ireland and 15 of them bravely entered the race along a 360-ft (110-m) trench. Casey wore a wetsuit and flippers, and a mask with a white lace veil.

RESTING PLACE
Jack Woodward's last wish was honored when his ashes were buried in the pub where he had spent many hours nearly every day of his life. The former landlord's remains lie beneath a flagstone in the bar at the Boat Inn pub in the village of Stoke Bruerne, Northamptonshire, England, with a plaque saying: "Stand here and have a drink on me."

HUMAN WEIGHTS
In January 2009, a fitness gym in London, England, set up weight-lifting machines using people as weights. The five differently sized human weights—ranging from a 66-lb (30-kg) man to a much heavier man weighing 340-lb (155-kg)—not only helped gym goers visualize the weight they were lifting, but the weights also shouted words of encouragement during their session.

EXPENSIVE HAIRCUT
The Sultan of Brunei, one of the richest men in the world, pays over $13,000 every month for a haircut. He pays the huge fee to fly his favorite barber, Ken Modestou, first-class, from London's Dorchester Hotel to Brunei and to have him stay in a hotel. Modestou normally charges $45 for a trim.

CANINE TUXEDO
Having first met while walking their dogs on the beach, Harriet and Andrew Athay of Dorset, England, chose their pet dog Ed to be best man at their wedding. Ed wore his own miniature tuxedo, while the couple's two female dogs, Humbug and Goulash, dressed in pink sparkly collars.

MILK ROUND
Eighty-one-year-old milkman Derek Arch has been delivering milk to homes in the city of Coventry, England, for nearly 70 years. Driving the same van he has had for more than 50 years, he rises at 2.30 a.m. to make his daily deliveries, seven days a week, visiting more than 400 houses and walking 8 mi (13 km) each day.

LLAMA GUARD
Two of farmer Terry McCrone's llamas served as the honor guard at his funeral in Plymouth Township, Ohio.

BEYOND REASON

TYPO SQUAD
As part of their campaign to eradicate bad spelling and punctuation, Jeff Deck of Somerville, Massachusetts, and Benjamin Herson of Virginia Beach, Virginia, toured the United States for two months in 2008, removing typographical errors from public signs.

WASP DIET
An eight-year-old Indian boy, Ravi Singh, is addicted to eating wasps. He says they have a sweet taste and he enjoys the sensation of the wasp's sting on his tongue. He can eat up to seven at a time and, although five wasp stings can kill a grown man, Ravi's body has developed a resistance to their poison.

LIFELIKE COSTUME
A man dressed as a gorilla for a charity run through England was stopped by police, who had received calls from passing motorists thinking he was a real ape that had escaped from a zoo! Rory Coleman was running to support the Gorilla Organization.

LIGHT RIDDLE
For five years, farmer Mo Zhaoguang from Nandan, Hubei Province, China, was mystified as to who kept turning on the light in his barn—until he finally realized it was his buffalo. Mo says the buffalo turns on the light when it is hungry or thirsty and then turns it off again afterward to go to sleep.

MOBILE ZOO
Police officers who stopped a motorist in Bari, Italy, found no fewer than 1,700 animals squeezed into the trunk of his car. Inside were more than 1,000 terrapins, 300 white mice, 216 budgies, 150 hamsters, 30 Japanese squirrels, and six chameleons.

GARBAGE COLLECTOR
Officials made Merv Jones move out of his home in Lincolnshire, England, while they cleared out 100 tons of rubbish that had been collected over decades and stacked floor-to-ceiling throughout the house. The stench from the waste, which included old ammunition, samurai swords, and propane gas canisters, was so bad that it could be smelled more than a mile away.

CANINE BRIDE
Two-year-old Sagula Munda was married to a dog at a ceremony in Jajpur, India, in 2009 to protect the boy from ghosts and further bad luck following the discovery of a rotten tooth in his gum.

USEFUL BONES
In 2009, seven years after his death, Gordon Krantz, a professor of osteology from Port Angeles, Washington State, received his dying wish that the bones of he and his dog become a museum display when he was exhibited in the Smithsonian Museum of Natural History.

CATTLE OFFER
During U.S. Secretary of State Hillary Clinton's 2009 visit to Kenya, 39-year-old Godwin Chepkurgor, a former Nairobi councilor, offered her 20 cows and 40 goats in exchange for the hand of her daughter Chelsea in marriage.

Dead Art
New York artist Nate Hill scours backstreet trashcans for animal carcasses, which he then sews together in unique, grotesque creations. Nate presented his grandest creation, the A.D.A.M. project, at his apartment in January 2008. A life-sized man with fish for shoulders and a deer-fur torso, A.D.A.M. is also part chicken, conch, cow, crab, duck, eel, frog, lobster, rabbit, and shark.

RIPLEY'S ask

Why did you start taxidermy art?
I started making taxidermy after I met a beautiful girl in college who was doing it. I wanted her to like me, so I used this thing she liked to get her attention. As I remember it, she was using a stapler to connect parts of different animals, and then submerging them in jars of rubbing alcohol. So I sewed together an opossum tail by hand and gave it to her. She liked it—but not enough to date me!

Where do you get your animals?
I get animals from everywhere possible, so it is a lot of places. They can be found in Chinatown fish markets and their garbage, Florida roadkill, live poultry houses in New York City, taxidermy supply websites, supermarket meats, sympathetic veterinary clinics, and probably more places.

What are the problems caused by using dead animals?
There are many problems. Exposure to disease and parasites is always a concern, but I have not had a problem yet. I store my animals in rubbing alcohol, and the fumes are not healthy to breathe. But the worst is the smell from the animals that are in the rubbing alcohol, which release a smell of rotting flesh into my life.

Cheesy Crawlies

Casu Marzu cheese is a gourmet tradition on the island of Sardinia, Italy. While many cheeses encourage the growth of bacteria, Casu Marzu is not ready to eat until it is fully infested with the maggot larvae of the cheese fly. As the maggots process the cheese, they give it the required moist texture, and then it is eaten, maggots and all. It is only when the maggots die that the cheese becomes unfit for human consumption.

ZOO QUEST
Marla Taviano and her family from Columbus, Ohio, visited 55 U.S. animal parks in 52 weeks. They began their 22,000-mi (35,405-km) safari at Louisville Zoo, Kentucky, in August 2008 and, after visits to zoos in Dallas, New York, and San Diego among others, ended it a year later at their hometown Columbus Zoo and Aquarium.

STOLEN SAND
Environmental enforcement officers supported by the Mexican Navy put crime tape around a Cancun hotel beach in 2009 on suspicion that the hotel had stolen the sand for its beach by pumping it illegally from the sea floor.

CROC JAILED
Police in Gunbalanya, Northern Territory, Australia, threw a 6½-ft-long (2-m) saltwater crocodile in jail for three days in October 2009 after it was found loitering in the town.

BIG BUBBLE
In August 2009, professional bubble maker Sam Heath (aka Samsam Bubbleman) of London, England, made a free-floating, multicolored soap bubble measuring 20 x 5 x 5 ft (6 x 1.5 x 1.5 m). He used a secret mixture—that he has spent 20 years perfecting—and a piece of rope tied between two sticks.

DOG BAN
A judge banned a small Pomeranian dog from the resort of Aspen, Colorado, in 2009 for repeatedly biting. Municipal Judge Brooke Peterson told the dog's owner that if the animal was seen again in Aspen, it would have to be put down. The dog, named Gizmo, had previously been sent to an animal shelter for ten days in a bid to curb its aggressive behavior.

RAPID BOUNCE
Ashrita Furman of New York City bounced a basketball 339 times in just 60 seconds in February 2009.

Carry on Canine
Irish customs officers were extremely surprised to see a Chihuahua dog clearly visible on the luggage X-ray screen at Dublin airport in October 2009. The dog had been smuggled out of Spain inside a passenger's hand luggage. Despite its unconventional method of travel, the dog was reported to be in good health.

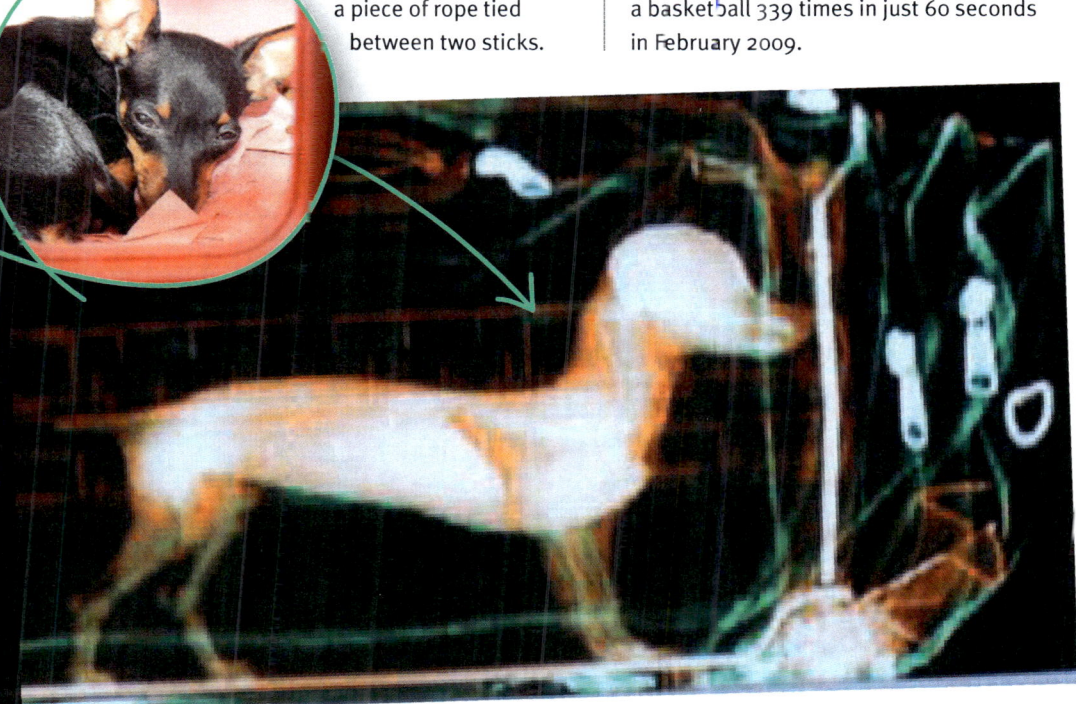

BEYOND REASON

Drinking Hole

A 46-year-old man woke up stuck from the waist down in a gully in Bochum, Germany, after a night of drinking in July 2009. With no knowledge of how he ended up jammed down the drain, the man was finally pulled out by baffled firefighters. Police are still confused as to how the drain cover was removed when he claims he did not touch it!

SNAKES BLAMED
A motorist who lost control of his sports utility vehicle in Hartford, Connecticut, in 2009 blamed the accident on two pet baby snakes that he said escaped from his pants pockets as he was driving. He claimed the snakes slithered near the gas and brake pedals and, while he and a passenger tried to catch them, the vehicle veered into some parked cars and overturned.

NEW NAME
After a night out, 19-year-old Tom Hayward, a computer-games design student from Leicestershire, England, changed his name by deed poll to N'Tom The Hayemaker Haywardyouliketocomebacktomine. He forgot all about it until he received a formal letter confirming his new name.

PRISONER RETURNS
Jail guards in Camden County, Georgia, caught a prisoner in March 2009 as he was sneaking back into jail after he had escaped to steal cigarettes from across the street.

UNDERPANTS SMUGGLER
In 2009, a man was caught wearing 15 pairs of contraband underpants, four tracksuits, and three pairs of pants as he tried to smuggle them into Belarus from Ukraine. He was sweating so heavily and waddling so badly that he could hardly walk, thus attracting the attention of customs officials.

THRIFTY BRIDE
Heather Saint, a 20-year-old bride from Teesside, England, beat the recession in 2008 by buying her wedding dress on the Internet auction site eBay for just five pence (8 cents).

PENGUIN MAN
For over 35 years, Alfred David of Brussels, Belgium, has lived life as a penguin. Monsieur le Penguin, as he is known, walks the streets in a penguin costume, likes to eat raw sardines, and preens himself to keep clean. He believes he has a telepathic connection with penguins, has a collection of more than 3,000 ornamental penguins, and has even hosted penguin exhibitions in Belgium and abroad. He wants to be buried in a penguin-shaped coffin and is convinced that he will eventually be reincarnated as a penguin.

JAWS BURGLAR
Police investigating a series of baffling burglaries through caged windows around Chongqing, China, discovered that the culprit had gained entry by biting through steel bars. When arrested, the man revealed that he could chew any steel bar up to 3/8 in (1 cm) thick by tearing open the welding spots with his powerful teeth.

BOMB ANCHOR
A fisherman in Johor, Malaysia, had been using an unexploded bomb from World War II as a boat anchor for months before he realized what it was.

PETTY CASH
When two women were laid off from their jobs at a ceilings-installation company in Vladivostok, Russia, their former boss paid them the $1,150 he owed them—in 33 heavy bags full of low-denomination coins.

VEGAS CRAZY
Anette and Kenneth Lund from Vejle, Denmark, got married four times in one day in 2008 in Las Vegas, Nevada. They wed in a hotel, in a limousine with the service conducted by an Elvis impersonator, in a helicopter, and while skydiving. They said they plan to get married once a year for the rest of their lives to keep their relationship exciting.

CLOWN STOLEN
An inflatable clown stolen from a Russian circus in Alice Springs, Northern Territory, Australia, in 2009 was found a few days later on a nearby golf course—along with a handwritten note in which he demanded better working conditions.

SLEEPING ON THE JOB
In 2009, Roisin Madigan, a student from Birmingham, England, was paid $1,500 to sleep in designer beds every day for a month. She spent eight hours a day in bed to help with a sleep survey being carried out by a luxury bed manufacturer.

Whale Watch

In July 2009, free diver Yang Yun was suffering dangerous paralyzing cramps when a Beluga whale, Mila, heroically guided her to the surface. Diving 20 ft (6 m) without any breathing equipment, Yun was facing certain death when her legs froze from the Arctic temperatures of the aquarium pool in Harbin, northeast China. Mila cleverly sensed the problem, well before the organizers did, and used her dolphin-like nose to push Yun to safety.

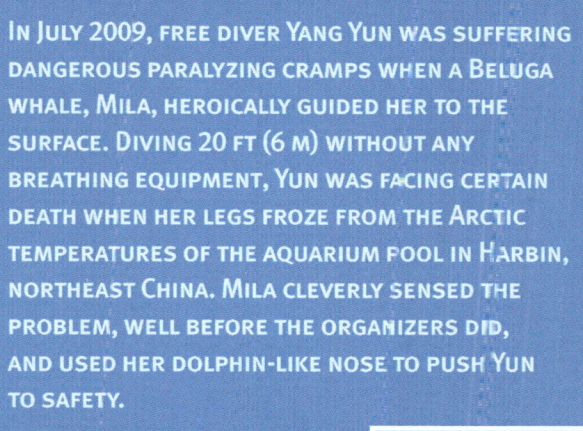

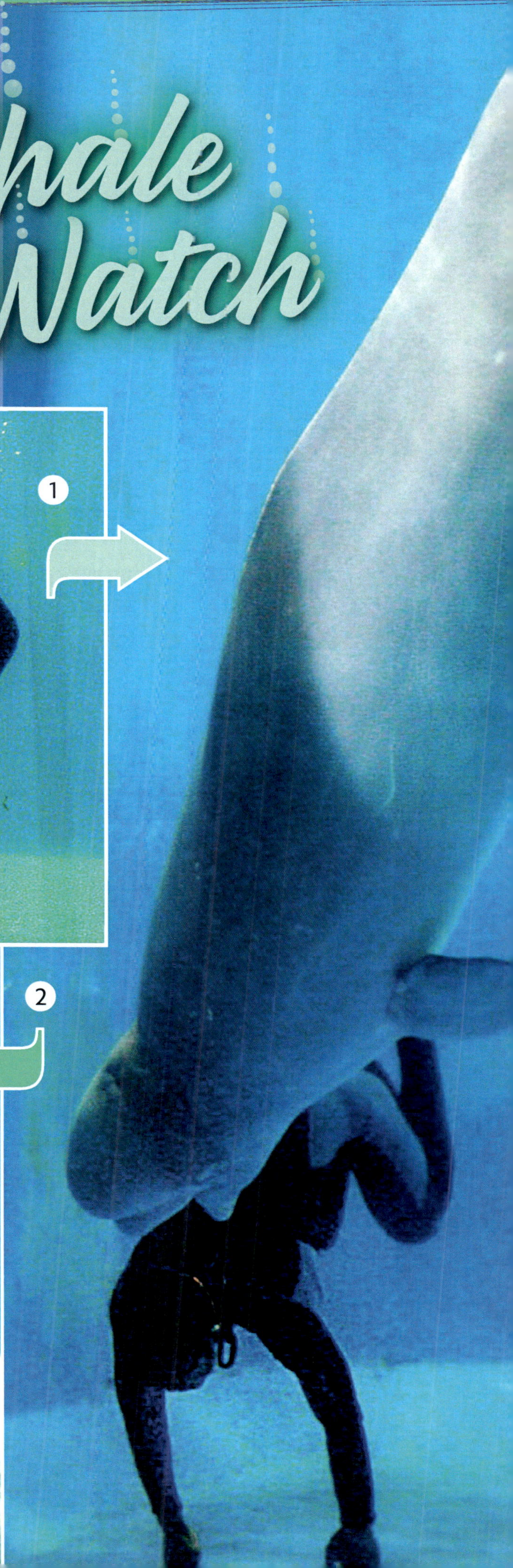

SPIDER SKIN

It might look like this man's skin has been scraped away to reveal a superhero suit, but it is actually a most extraordinary life-like tattoo by Dan Hazelton from Milwaukee, Wisconsin. The talented skin artist inked the startling design, known as a "tear out," on a tattoo-mad client's chest in 1996. The design took ten hours of work over three sessions.

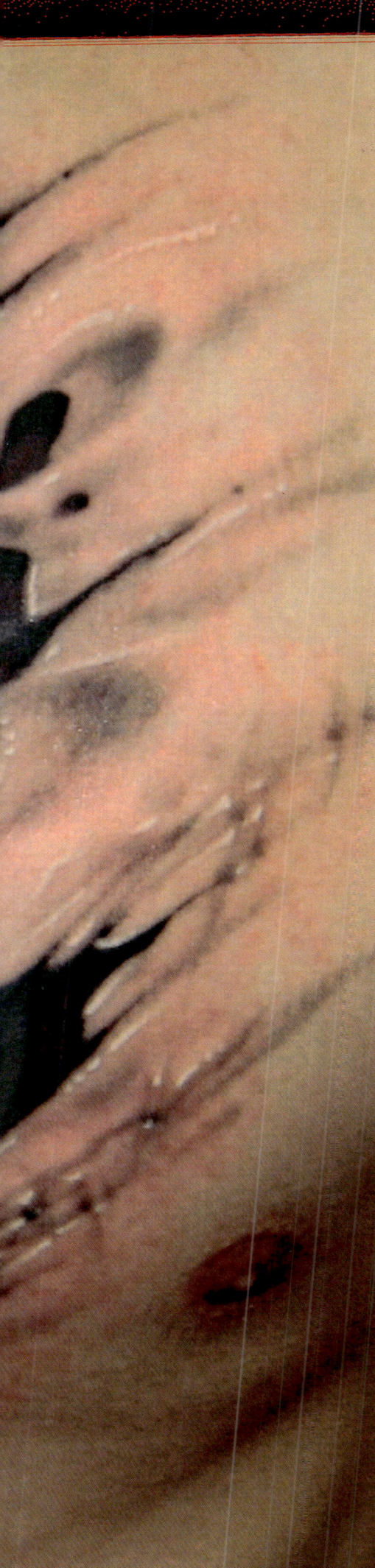

SAME TIE
Attorney Bob Flournoy of Lufkin, Texas, wore the same U.S. flag tie every day for more than six years. With daily wear, the tie started to disintegrate, forcing Bob to cut portions out and hold it together with Velcro, but by 2007 it was only half its original size and was too fragile even to tie.

GNOME RESCUE
When an elderly Australian lady died in 2009, the 1,500 ornamental gnomes she had collected over the years faced eviction from their home in Cootamundra, New South Wales, and the prospect of being thrown in a dumpster. However, local people came to the rescue and in a four-hour operation they rounded up the gnomes with a view to finding foster homes for them.

BAMBOO BALANCE
Three couples got married on the Xiangjiang River in Zunyi City, China, in January 2009 while balancing on bamboo poles that measured 8 in (20 cm) in diameter. The couples, who wore traditional wedding attire, are all members of the local single bamboo rafting club and chose to get married on the water to demonstrate their skill at the sport.

FAST-FOOD CEREMONY
Paul and Caragh Brooks got married in Normal, Illinois, in 2009 in their favorite restaurant—a branch of the Mexican fast-food chain Taco Bell.

FRIDGE PARTY
Paul and Val Howkins from Coventry, England, invited friends and family to a 50th birthday party—for their fridge. They had banners, party poppers, and even a cake to celebrate the milestone birthday of the still-working fridge, which they bought for around $100 in 1959.

CHAMELEON CHAOS
A fire brigade in Hampshire, England, sent 18 officers, three trucks, and a unit wearing special chemical protective clothing to a house in Basingstoke—to clean up a broken jar containing a pickled chameleon that had been preserved in formaldehyde.

QUIT SMOKING
After smoking for 95 years, 102-year-old Winnie Langley from London, England, finally decided to quit in 2009. Since her first puff in 1914, she smoked on average five cigarettes a day, making a total of more than 170,000.

CAT CALLS
Police broke into a home in Sussex, England, after a cat dialed the emergency number 999 four times in the space of a few minutes. The owner, who was perfectly safe and well the whole time, said her cat Watson, who enjoys playing with the phone, must have accidentally called the number.

ROBOT DANCERS
A total of 269 people dressed as robots on the Bournemouth and Poole College campus, in Dorset, England, in July 2009 and gave a five-minute performance of robot dancing.

THREE POLES
British explorer Adrian Hayes reached the three extreme points of the Earth—the North and South Poles and the summit of Mount Everest—in the space of just 19 months. He climbed to the top of Everest in May 2006, arrived at the North Pole in April 2007, and reached the South Pole in December 2007—a daunting triple challenge that takes most explorers several years to attempt.

BARE HANDS
On November 21, 2008, expert knife thrower the Rev. Dr. David Adamovich—aka The Great Throwdini—from Freeport, New York, caught a thrown knife, a flying arrow, and a fired .22 caliber bullet—all with his bare hands.

CLOVER BUNCH
Ten-year-old Mabel South picked more than 120 four-leafed clovers in the garden of her home in Hertfordshire, England, in less than half an hour. The bunch included three five-leafed clovers and one six-leafed clover.

BLINDFOLD SKATER
Nine-year-old limbo skater Rohan Ajit Kokane squeezed his body under a car with a clearance height of just 6 3/4 in (17.1 cm) at Belgaum, India, in 2009—while blindfolded.

SOLO SAILOR
Southern Californian sailor Zac Sunderland completed a 13-month, 28,000-mile (45,000-km) solo voyage around the world in July 2009—at age 17. Zac, who was just 16 when he set off from Marina del Rey in June 2008, endured many dramas on his 36-ft (11-m) boat Intrepid, not least during the leg from Australia to the Coco Islands when he was followed by pirates and forced to call the Australian authorities to scare them off.

BEYOND REASON

Lean Machine
In Huai'an City, in East China's Jiangsu Province, a truck driver checks that his bundles of goods are still secure.

IRREGULAR BIKE
Guan Baihua of Qingdao, China, spent 18 months developing a bicycle with odd-shaped wheels. The front wheel is a five-sided pentagon, while the back wheel is a triangle. He says the bike is mainly for fun but adds that riders could use it to lose weight because it takes more effort to pedal.

PUMPKIN HELMETS
After new laws were brought in to force Nigerian motorcyclists to wear helmets, a number of bikers in the northern city of Kano were spotted wearing dried pumpkin shells on their heads.

UNEXPECTED PASSENGER
A delivery man driving a small van near Peddie, Eastern Cape, South Africa, in May 2009 collided with a bull and had to drive around 9 mi (14 km) to a local police station—with the animal still wedged in the vehicle's roof rack.

EMERGENCY LANDING
A small airplane bound for Santa Barbara Airport, California, was hit by three cars after making an emergency landing on a nearby highway. The Piper PA-24 Comanche, with two people on board, touched down a mile from the airport on U.S. Highway 101 after running out of fuel. Although nine people were involved in the accident, nobody was hurt.

TOILET LANDING
A pilot escaped unhurt in May 2009 when his small airplane's crash landing was cushioned by a pile of portable toilets. After taking off from an airfield near Tacoma, Washington State, the Cessna 182's engine failed at a height of about 160 ft (50 m). As it dropped from the sky, it hit a fence, flipped over, and landed upside down on top of portable toilets stacked in a storage yard.

REPEAT OFFENDER
A man in Boynton Beach, Florida, received more than 50 traffic citations from police in one day on February 5, 2009.

FARE CHOICE
At Recession Ride Taxi in Essex, Vermont, proprietor Eric Hagen allows his passengers to decide how much they want to pay. Most pay cash, but he has also received a CD from a musician and a $10 supermarket card—and he hasn't been short-changed yet.

Donkey Wreath
Doing all the hard work, a donkey is guided along a road south of Dushanbe, Tajikistan, carrying hundreds of leaves on his back.

KARAOKE CAB
Fan Xiaoming of Changchun, Jilin, China, has fitted out his taxi cab with media players, an amplifier, speakers, LCD screens, and a microphone—so his passengers can sing along on their journeys.

UNLUCKY DAY
Former U.S. President Franklin D. Roosevelt was so superstitious that he always avoided travel on the 13th day of each month.

TOWED AWAY
Ruth Ducker of London, England, was told she would have to pay more than $3,000 to reclaim her illegally parked car—after local council workers lifted it up, painted double yellow "no-parking" lines under it and then towed it away.

STILL GOING
Seventy percent of Land Rover all-terrain vehicles—first built in the U.K. in 1948—are still on the road.

Riding Recycler
A woman in Shanghai carries masses of Styrofoam for recycling on the back of her bicycle.

Coco-Nutter

IN MYSORE, INDIA, A COCONUT GATHERER TRANSPORTS HIS HUSKS TO THE LOCAL MARKET ON HIS THREE-WHEELED RICKSHAW.

Traveling by Air
In Tianjin, China, a cyclist travels under a cloud of bright pink and red helium balloons.

Motor-Hog
Two men in Moung Russey, Cambodia, carry a large pig on the back of their motorbike.

℞ LIFE BAN
In January 2009, a court banned 84-year-old Luba Relic of Warriewood, New South Wales, Australia, from driving until the year 3000.

℞ STRANGE HYBRID
Friends Nicolo Lamberti and Milko Dalla Costa took the chassis of a speedy Ferrari F355 Berlinetta and crossed it with the body of a Citroën 2CV bread van—and created a bread van capable of speeds of 180 mph (290 km/h). After discovering the Citroën in Turate, Italy, the pair spent five years and more than $220,000 putting together their bizarre hybrid.

℞ FOLDING BIKE
Dominic Hargreaves, a graduate from the Royal College of Art in London, England, has devised a bicycle that folds up to be smaller than its own wheels. He sees "the Contortionist" as being the perfect bike for commuters because when folded it can be wheeled along the street by one handlebar.

www.ripleybooks.com

Smelly Nelly

In August 2009, a baby elephant was walking to work with his trainer in Rayong Province in Thailand when he slipped and fell into a manhole. His owner had taken his eyes off him for just a moment when he turned to find the calf stuck in the 3-ft-wide (90-cm) drain. It took three hours for rescuers to get him out, eventually having to use a bulldozer to widen the hole. The elephant miraculously survived without any injuries.

UNBELIEVABLE OFFER
A four-star hotel near Venice, Italy, lost $129,000 after mistakenly offering a romantic weekend for just one cent. The Crowne Plaza received over 1,400 room reservations as soon as the offer—the result of a human error at their head office in Atlanta, Georgia—was posted on its website.

YOUNG LECTURER
Aman Rehman of Dehradun in Uttarakhand state, India, started teaching adult students computer-generated animated film at Dehradun's College of Interactive Arts in 2009—when he was just eight years old! The son of an illiterate mechanic, Aman mastered his first animation program at age three and a half and has since made more than 1,000 animated films.

ELECTION DRAW
When a 2009 council election in Cave Creek, Arizona, ended in a tie, the result was decided by invoking a 1925 local statute and drawing from a deck of cards. Adam Trenk was elected after his king of hearts beat rival candidate Thomas McGuire's six of hearts.

BUNGEE HORROR
Australian backpacker Erin Langworthy miraculously survived following a 364-ft-fall (111-m) into the crocodile-infested waters of the Zambezi River after the cord snapped while she was bungee jumping from a bridge between Zambia and Zimbabwe. Although her feet were still tied together as she plunged head first into the rapids, the 22-year-old managed to swim to shore.

HUMAN KEBAB

A wayward throw from a classmate left athlete Jian Liao writhing in agony on the track at Guilin, China, as a 5-ft (1.5-m) javelin went through his kneecap. Rescue workers tried to cut the spear off with bolt cutters, but when Jian screamed in pain, they set fire to it instead and burned it in half before they moved him.

INCRIMINATING POOP

Swedish police solved a robbery by tracing the two robbers through their excrement. The pair had stopped for a poop outside a strawberry farm near Vara, Sweden, before breaking in, tying up the owner, and stealing cash and his car. However, while they remembered to torch the stolen vehicle, they forgot to scoop the poop, allowing detectives to extract vital DNA from it.

DEAD COOL

For the wake of Treme Brass Band drummer "Uncle" Lionel Batiste at a funeral home in New Orleans, Louisiana, on July 19, 2012, his dead body was embalmed, dressed in his finest clothes, and propped up against a faux street lamp, his hands resting on his trademark cane.

POLICE INTELLIGENCE

Zealous police officers from Surrey, England, raided a village pub which was advertising live music from "4am," only to find that was the name of the band. The two-piece band, composed of Joe Becket and John Adams, chose the name based on a track by jazz musician Herbie Hancock.

HARLEY HEARSE

By attaching a sidecar hearse to a Harley Davidson, Joerg Grossmann from Frankfurt, Germany, has created the perfect funeral for die-hard bikers who want to ride until the very end.

BURIAL PROTEST

In a protest against property developers who overnight chopped down the 4,000-tree forest he had planted over a 30-year period on the edge of his village, environmentalist Zhou Haijue of Guangdong Province, China, dug a large hole in the ground and buried himself up to his neck until government officials agreed to recognize his claim to the land.

BIGGEST CATCH

While on a sea fishing trip, a Polish angler landed the biggest catch of his life when he accidentally hooked his 210-lb (95-kg) friend in the mouth. Fifty-year-old Bogdan Symanski felt a sudden tug on his mouth, followed by blinding pain and spurting blood.

KITCHEN DIG

To reach an underground river full of fish, Li Huiyan of Chongqing, China, hired 30 villagers to dig a 50-ft (16-m) hole in his kitchen. After digging down to the river, he placed a fishing net across it and hauled out enough fish every day to support his family.

SCRAP YARD

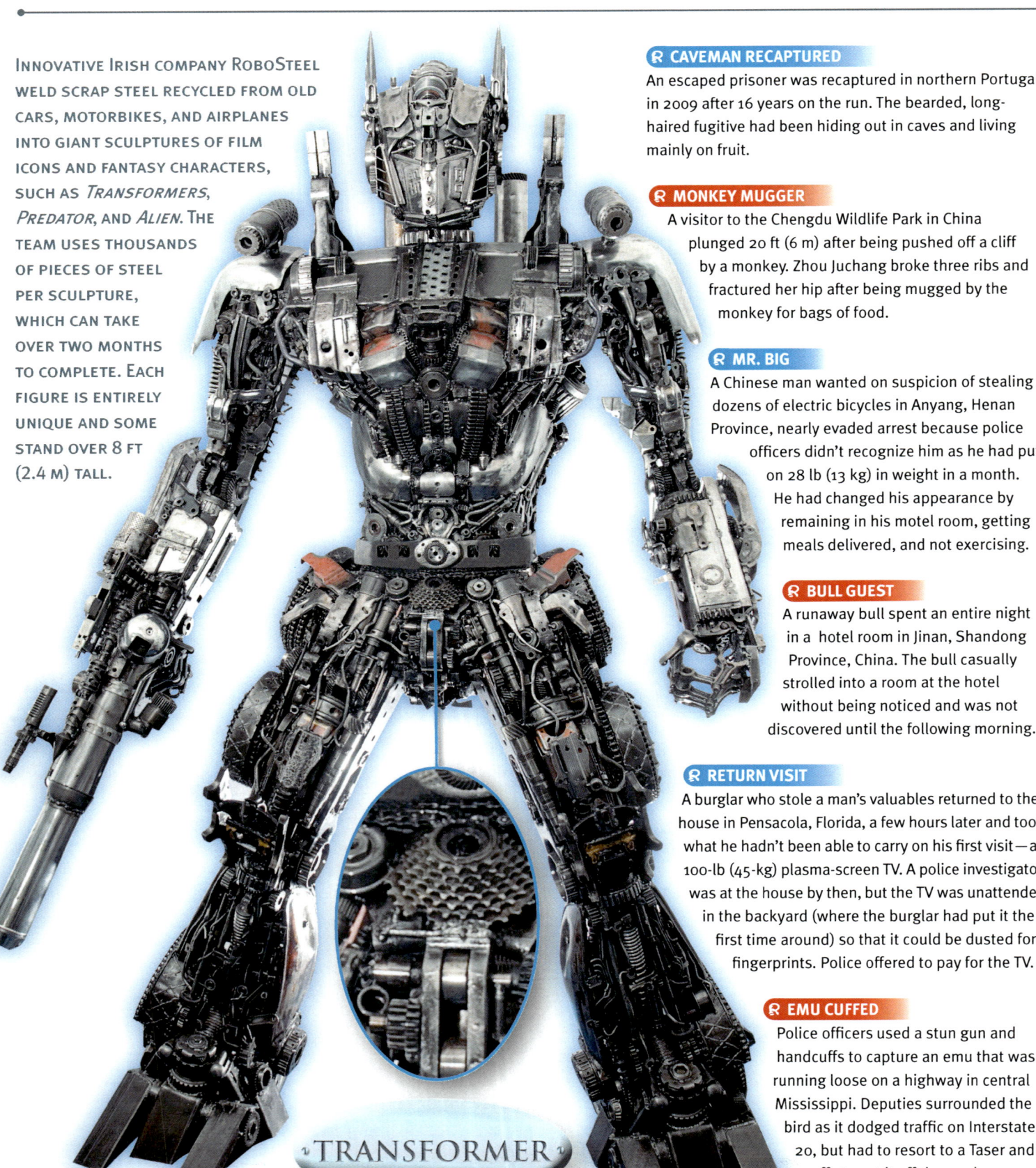

TRANSFORMER

Innovative Irish company RoboSteel weld scrap steel recycled from old cars, motorbikes, and airplanes into giant sculptures of film icons and fantasy characters, such as *Transformers*, *Predator*, and *Alien*. The team uses thousands of pieces of steel per sculpture, which can take over two months to complete. Each figure is entirely unique and some stand over 8 ft (2.4 m) tall.

CAVEMAN RECAPTURED
An escaped prisoner was recaptured in northern Portugal in 2009 after 16 years on the run. The bearded, long-haired fugitive had been hiding out in caves and living mainly on fruit.

MONKEY MUGGER
A visitor to the Chengdu Wildlife Park in China plunged 20 ft (6 m) after being pushed off a cliff by a monkey. Zhou Juchang broke three ribs and fractured her hip after being mugged by the monkey for bags of food.

MR. BIG
A Chinese man wanted on suspicion of stealing dozens of electric bicycles in Anyang, Henan Province, nearly evaded arrest because police officers didn't recognize him as he had put on 28 lb (13 kg) in weight in a month. He had changed his appearance by remaining in his motel room, getting meals delivered, and not exercising.

BULL GUEST
A runaway bull spent an entire night in a hotel room in Jinan, Shandong Province, China. The bull casually strolled into a room at the hotel without being noticed and was not discovered until the following morning.

RETURN VISIT
A burglar who stole a man's valuables returned to the house in Pensacola, Florida, a few hours later and took what he hadn't been able to carry on his first visit—a 100-lb (45-kg) plasma-screen TV. A police investigator was at the house by then, but the TV was unattended in the backyard (where the burglar had put it the first time around) so that it could be dusted for fingerprints. Police offered to pay for the TV.

EMU CUFFED
Police officers used a stun gun and handcuffs to capture an emu that was running loose on a highway in central Mississippi. Deputies surrounded the bird as it dodged traffic on Interstate 20, but had to resort to a Taser and cuffs to get it off the road.

MONSTERS

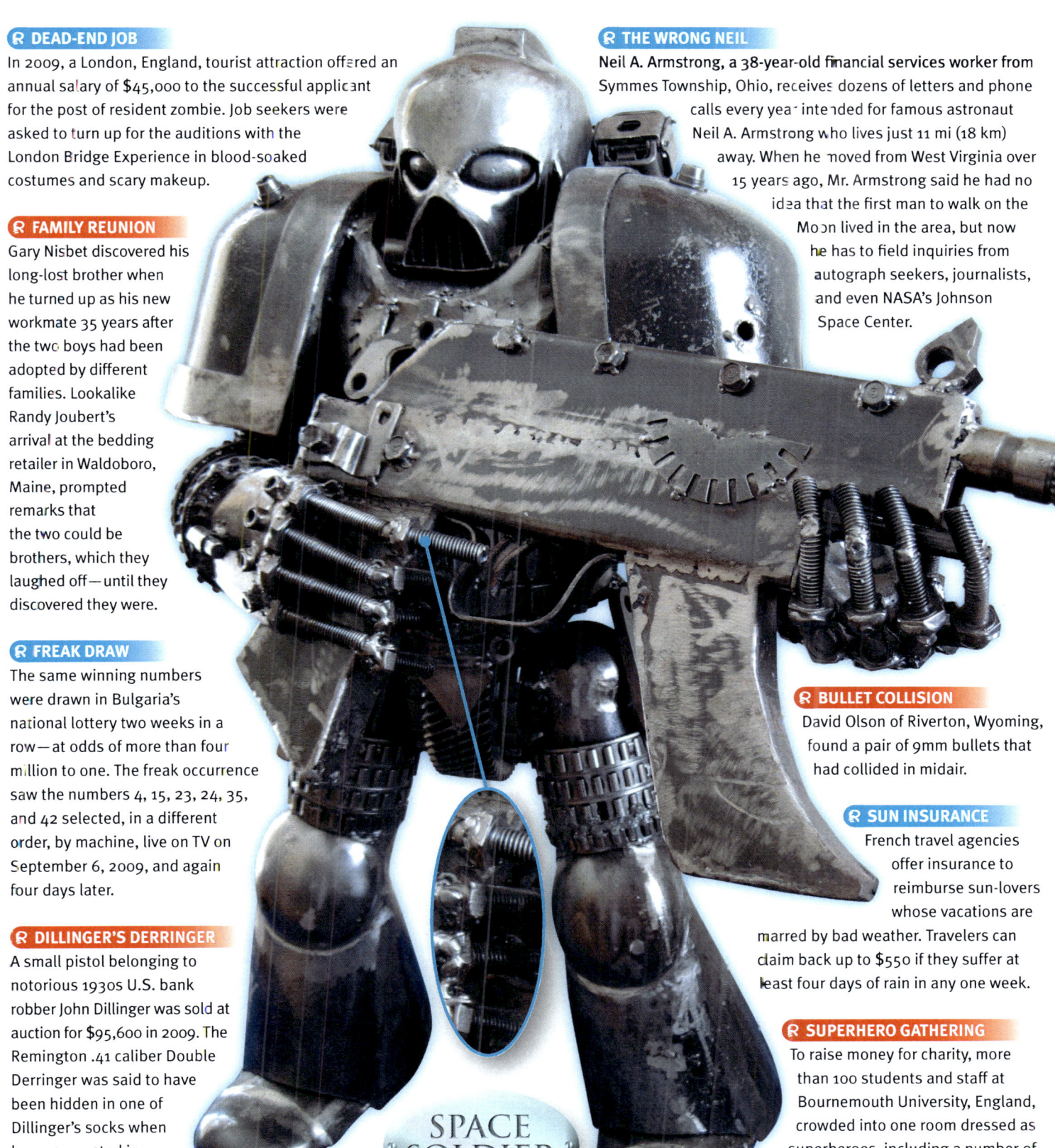

SPACE SOLDIER

R DEAD-END JOB
In 2009, a London, England, tourist attraction offered an annual salary of $45,000 to the successful applicant for the post of resident zombie. Job seekers were asked to turn up for the auditions with the London Bridge Experience in blood-soaked costumes and scary makeup.

R FAMILY REUNION
Gary Nisbet discovered his long-lost brother when he turned up as his new workmate 35 years after the two boys had been adopted by different families. Lookalike Randy Joubert's arrival at the bedding retailer in Waldoboro, Maine, prompted remarks that the two could be brothers, which they laughed off—until they discovered they were.

R FREAK DRAW
The same winning numbers were drawn in Bulgaria's national lottery two weeks in a row—at odds of more than four million to one. The freak occurrence saw the numbers 4, 15, 23, 24, 35, and 42 selected, in a different order, by machine, live on TV on September 6, 2009, and again four days later.

R DILLINGER'S DERRINGER
A small pistol belonging to notorious 1930s U.S. bank robber John Dillinger was sold at auction for $95,600 in 2009. The Remington .41 caliber Double Derringer was said to have been hidden in one of Dillinger's socks when he was arrested in 1934 in Tucson, Arizona.

R THE WRONG NEIL
Neil A. Armstrong, a 38-year-old financial services worker from Symmes Township, Ohio, receives dozens of letters and phone calls every year intended for famous astronaut Neil A. Armstrong who lives just 11 mi (18 km) away. When he moved from West Virginia over 15 years ago, Mr. Armstrong said he had no idea that the first man to walk on the Moon lived in the area, but now he has to field inquiries from autograph seekers, journalists, and even NASA's Johnson Space Center.

R BULLET COLLISION
David Olson of Riverton, Wyoming, found a pair of 9mm bullets that had collided in midair.

R SUN INSURANCE
French travel agencies offer insurance to reimburse sun-lovers whose vacations are marred by bad weather. Travelers can claim back up to $550 if they suffer at least four days of rain in any one week.

R SUPERHERO GATHERING
To raise money for charity, more than 100 students and staff at Bournemouth University, England, crowded into one room dressed as superheroes, including a number of Batmen and Supermen.

INDEX

Page numbers in *italics* refer to illustrations

A
Abreu, Emerson de Oliveira (Bra) 7
Adamovich, Rev. Dr. David (U.S.A.) 27
Adams, Joanne (U.K.) 14
airplanes 8, 9, 23, *23*, 28
Albu, Elena (Rom) 18
alcohol, in hand gel 18
Alder, Alec (U.K.) 18
Allen, Lou (U.K.) 10
anchor, bomb used as 24
Anderson, Jolene (Aus) 13, *13*
animal parks, visiting 23
animator, very young 30
Arch, Derek (U.K.) 21
Armstrong, Neil A. (U.S.A.) 33
arrows, catching in hand 27
astronauts 9, *9*, 16, 18, 33
Athay, Harriet and Andrew (U.K.) 21

B
bachelorette party 21
bacon, dress made of 13, *13*
ball, giant matzo 14
balloons 8, 29, *29*
band, police raid pub because of 31
bars 16
basketball, multiple bounces 23
Batiste, Lionel (U.S.A.) 31
beach, hotel steals sand for 23
beards 7
beer 12, 16
Belden, Judge Stephen (U.S.A.) 21
Bertoletti, Patrick (U.S.A.) 14
bicycles 28, *28*, 29, *29*
birds 18, 24, 32
birthday party, for fridge 27
Blanche of Navarre (Fra) 12
Blazova, Jana (Svk) 13
blindfolded, limbo skating under car 27
BLT sandwich, enormous 12
boats and ships 8, 24, 27
bogsnorkelling 21
bomb, used as anchor 24
Bompas, Sam (U.K.) 12
Bonds, Briana (U.S.A.) 7
books, in road tarmac 9
brandy, effect on nose 11, *11*
breweries, German 12
Brock, George and Leslie (U.S.A.) 11
Brooks, Paul and Caragh (U.S.A.) 27
brothers, long-lost 33
Brown, Harry (U.S.A.) 21
Brunei, Sultan of 21
bubble, enormous 23
buffalo, turns lights on 22
Buford, Craig (U.S.A.) 13
bugs, eating 15, *15*
building, fire truck on top of 9
bullets 7, 19, *19*, 27, 33
bulls 28, 32
bungee jump, into crocodile-infested waters 30
burglars 24
butt, needle removed from 7

C
calamari, speed-eating 14
Camejo, Luis Enrique (Cub) 10
Cammarata, Angelo (U.S.A.) 16
candies, grasshoppers in 15
cars
  cardboard cutouts of police cars 8
  child drives 8
  coyote stuck in fender 21, *21*
  elderly driver banned 29
  fridge looks like 10, *10*
  huge number of animals in 22
  illegally parked 28
  limbo skating under 27
  long-lasting 28
  long lost 9
  lottery ticket replica of 8, *8*
  multiple traffic citations 28
  snakes cause accident 24
  surviving crashes 18
  very small 8
cassava, poison 12
cat, dials emergency number 27
centenarian, gives up smoking 27
cheese 12, 23, *23*
cheesecake, giant 16
chef, lives in freezer 11
Chepkurgor, Godwin (Ken) 22
chicken 12
children, abandoned 20
chili peppers 16, 17, *17*
chocolate 10, 12
chowder festival 15
clams 11, 15
Clarke, Simon (U.K.) 15
Clinton, Hillary and Chelsea (U.S.A.) 22
clothes 13, *13*, 24
Clough, Lucy (U.K.) 11
clover, four-leafed 27
clowns 18, 24
coffin, fridge looks like 10, *10*
coins, women paid in 24
Coleman, Rory (U.K.) 22
computer, cremation ashes in 18
corpses, restaurant serves edible body parts 10
coyote, stuck in car fender 21, *21*
cream tea, enormous 15
cremation ashes 18, 20, *20*, 21
crocodiles 8, 23
Culp, Connie (U.S.A.) 7
curry, very expensive 12

D
Dalla Costa, Milko (Ita) 29
dancing, robot 27
Darwin, Charles (U.K.) 7
David, Alfred (Bel) 24
death 7, 18
Deck, Jeff (U.S.A.) 22
Dillinger, John (U.S.A.) 33
diver, whale saves 25, *25*
divorce, house sawn in half after 18
dogs
  banned from town 23
  best man at wedding 21
  child married to 22
  smuggled on plane 23, *23*
  very expensive 20
donkey, carries huge load 28
drains 20, 24, *24*, 30, *30*
duck embryos, eating 14, *14*
Ducker, Ruth (U.K.) 28
dumbbells, mortars used as 18
Durrant, Dean (U.K.) 13

E
eBay, wedding dress bought on 24
Eckstrom, Adam (U.S.A.) 8, *8*
eclair, giant 10
election, playing cards decide 30
elephants 30, *30*
embalmed body at wake 31
emu, police capture 32
England, Christine (U.K.) 18
Entwistle, Thomas (U.K.) 7
Essen, Quentin von (Aus) 10
Everest, Mount 27

F
Fabelo, Roberto (Cub) 10
face
  bullet removed from 19, *19*
  piece of glass found in chin 7
  transplant 7
Fan Xiaoming (Chn) 28
fat, huge amount removed 7
Feeney, Simone and Ryan (U.K.) 21
feet, writing with 13
Fewins, Tom (U.K.) 8
fire brigade, cleans up pickled chameleon 27
fire truck, on top of building 9
fish 15, 31
fishing, hooked man 31
flags 6, *6*, 27
Flournoy, Bob (U.S.A.) 27
food
  prison serves very good 15
  rotten food makes people ill 12
  speed-eating 14, 17, *17*
  unusual items 12, *12*, 15, *15*, 22
freezer, chef lives in 11
fridges 10, *10*, 12, 27
frogs 14, *14*, 15
funeral, llamas as honor guard 21
Furman, Ashrita (U.S.A.) 23

G
garlic, eating chocolate-covered 12
Gates, Bill (U.S.A.) 7
gnomes, large collection of 27
goats, offered for Chelsea Clinton's hand in marriage 22
Gonzalez, Mario Miguel (Cub) 10
gorilla, running in costume 22
grasshoppers, candies filled with 15
Green, Keith (U.K.) 18
Grossmann, Joerg (Ger) 31
Guan Baihua (Chn) 28
guns 7, 13, 33

H
Hagen, Eric (U.S.A.) 28
hair
  body covered in 7, *7*
  giant hairball in stomach 18, *18*
  very expensive haircut 21
hallucinations, fish cause 15
hand gel, alcohol content 18
hands
  catching arrows in 27
  cracking knuckles 18
  giant fingers 19, *19*
Hargreaves, Dominic (U.K.) 29
Harley Davidson hearse 31
Hawking, Stephen (U.K.) 7
Hayes, Adrian (U.K.) 27
Hayward, Tom (U.K.) 24
Hazelton, Dan (U.S.A.) 26, *26*
head, spear in 7
Heard, Michaela (U.K.) 10
hearse, sidecar as 31
heart, in wrong place 15
Heath, Sam (U.K.) 23
helicopter, home-made 9
Herson, Benjamin (U.S.A.) 22
Hill, Nate (U.S.A.) 22, *22*
hole, man buried himself in 31
hospitals 16, 20
hotels
  bull in 32
  steals sand for beach 23
  suite for pigeons 18
  very cheap offer 30
Hou Guoying (Chn) 19, *19*
houses
  rubbish cleared from 22
  sawn in half after divorce 18
Howkins, Paul and Val (U.K.) 27

I
insects 12, 15
insults, free beer for 16
International Space Station 16, 18
IQ, child with high 7

J

javelin, through knee 31, *31*
jello, glows in dark 12
Jem, Jia (U.S.A.) 13, *13*
Jian Liao (Chn) 31, *31*
Jones, Merv (U.K.) 22
Joubert, Randy (U.S.A.) 33
judge, orders defendant's mouth to be taped shut 21

K

karaoke, in taxi 28
kebabs, mice 16, *16*
King, Natalie (U.K.) 16
knives, catching in hand 27
knuckles, cracking 18
Kobozevsa, Lilia and Liana (Rus) 18
Kokane, Rohan Ajit (Ind) 27
Krantz, Gordon (U.S.A.) 22

L

Laliberté, Guy (Can) 18
Lamberti, Nicolo (Ita) 29
Langdon, Professor (U.K.) 7, *7*
Langley, Winnie (U.K.) 27
Langworthy, Erin (Aus) 30
Lao Du (Chn) 7
legs, eight-legged frog 14, *14*
lettuce, effect on rabbits 12
Li Huiyan (Chn) 31
lights, buffalo turns on 22
limbo skating, under car 27
Linley, Claire and Stuart (U.K.) 21
Liu Ge (Chn) 11, *11*
Liu Hua (Chn) 19, *19*
llamas, honor guard at funeral 21
lobster roll, giant 11
Lockwood, Lara (U.K.) 8
lollipops, with worms in 15
Lopes, Joan (U.K.) 11
lotteries 8, *8*, 33
Lovering family (U.K.) 15
Lund, Anette and Kenneth (Den) 24

M

McCrone, Terry (U.S.A.) 21
McGinlay, Sean (U.K.) 16
McGuire, Thomas (U.S.A.) 30
Madigan, Roisin (U.K.) 24
maggots, eating in cheese 23, *23*
mail boat, has own zip code 8
Mamoyac, Derek (U.S.A.) 12
manhole covers, stolen 20
map, tattooed 6, *6*
marriage proposals 23, *22*
Mars, soil fertility 12
matzo ball, giant 14
meat, dress made of 13, *13*
memory, garlic to improve 12
mice, kebabs 16, *16*
milkman, very long career 21

Mo Zhaoguang (Chn) 22
Modestou, Ken (U.K.) 21
money 7, 24
monkey, pushes woman off cliff 32
mortars, used as dumbbells 18
motorcycles 18, 28, 29, *29*
mountains 12, 27
movies, *Shrek* wedding 18
Munda, Sagula (Ind) 22
Munoz, Annie (Pan) 15
mustaches 18

N

name, changing 24
Narayan, Rakesh "Cobra" 12
Nebraska, abandoned children 20
needle, removed from butt cheek 7
Nisbet, Gary (U.S.A.) 33
North Pole 27
nose, very wide 11, *11*

O

Oakley, Karina (U.K.) 7
olives, crop stolen 10
Olson, David (U.S.A.) 33

P

pancakes 10, 16
Parr, Harry (U.K.) 12
peaches, sculpture made from 13, *13*
pearl, found in clam 11
penguin, living life as 24
Pereira, Ivonete (Bra) 7
Perruorria, Jorge (Cub) 10
Peterson, Brooke (U.S.A.) 23
Philippe Auguste, King of France 12
pig, on motorcycle 29, *29*
pigeons, hotel suite for 18
Pinkard, April (U.S.A.) 15
pizzas 10, 11, 16
playing cards, decide election 30
poison 12, 15, 22
police
  bonuses for mustaches 18
  catch robbers using excrement 31
  raid pub by mistake 31
police cars, cardboard cutouts of 8
potato chips, living on 14
prisons
  crocodile imprisoned 23
  inmates drink hand gel 18
  long time on the run from 32
  prisoner caught returning to 24
  serves very good food 15
pub, cremation ashes buried in 21
pumpkins, as helmets 28

R

rabbits, effect of lettuce on 12
rain, insuring vacations 33
Rehman, Aman (Ind) 30
Relic, Luba (Aus) 29
restaurants
  chef lives in freezer 11
  hospital-themed 16
  purple pearl found in clam 11
  serves chicken poisoned by snake 12
  serves edible body parts 10
  spy-themed 10
  very expensive curry 12
  wedding in 27
"Rham Sam" 7, *7*
rickshaw, large load on 29, *29*
riots, controling with chili 16
Rishi, Guinness (Ind) 6, *6*
roads 9, 28
robberies 7, 20, 31, 32
Robbins, Billy (U.S.A.) 7
robot dancing, display of 27
Roosevelt, Eleanor (U.S.A.) 12
Roosevelt, Franklin D. (U.S.A.) 28
rugby, players eat huge meals 16
running, in gorilla costume 22

S

Saint, Heather (U.K.) 24
salami, dress made of 13, *13*
sand, hotel steals for beach 23
sandwich, enormous BLT 12
sausage, giant 16
Savelyev, Sergey (Rus) 21
scone, enormous 15
scream, very loud 21
sculpture
  made from peaches 13, *13*
  scrap metal 32, *32*, 33
  taxidermy as 22, *22*
Semyonova, Alexei and Dmitry (Rus) 18
shower, truck driver takes 8
Shrek-themed wedding 18
signs, removing errors from 22
silkworm, eating pupae 12, *12*
Singh, Ravi (Ind) 22
skating, limbo skating under car 27
skeleton, displayed in museum 22
sleep survey 24
smoking, centenarian gives up 27
smuggling 23, *23*, 24
snakes 12, 24
soap bubble, enormous 23
soil, on Mars 12
soup, chowder festival 15
South, Mabel (U.K.) 27
South Pole 27
space tourist, dressed as clown 18
spelling, checking signs 22

spider tattoo 26, *26*
Spooner, Alison (U.K.) 13
spy-themed restaurant 10
Squibb, Casey (U.K.) 21
stomach, giant hairball in 18, *18*
Sunderland, Zac (U.S.A.) 27
superheroes, mass gathering of 33
superstitions, President's 28
surgery 7, 13
Symanski, Bogdan (Pol) 31

T

tall people 7
tarmac, books in 9
Tattersall, Anne (U.K.) 15
tattoos 6, *6*, 26, *26*
Taviano, Maria (U.S.A.) 23
taxidermy, as art 22, *22*
taxis 28
telephone, cat dials emergency number 27
tie, wearing same for years 27
tinned food, unusual items 12, *12*
toasters 11, 21
toilets, plane crashes onto 28
traffic citations, multiple 28
trains 9, *9*, 18
Tran, Dennis (U.S.A.) 16
transplants, face 7
travel, round world without using airplanes 8
Trenk, Adam (U.S.A.) 30
trucks 8, 9, 28, *28*
tumor, enormous 13
turkey, stuffed with smaller birds 14
twins 13, 18
Tyson, Mike (U.S.A.) 18

U

Unger, Donald L. (U.S.A.) 18
urine, recycling into water 16

V

vacations, insuring against bad weather 33
van, very fast 29
Van Duzer, Scott (U.S.A.) 10
Vance, Chad (U.S.A.) 18

W

wake, embalmed body at 31
Wang, Mrs. (Chn) 20
Wang Houju (Chn) 13
Was, Lauren (U.S.A.) 8, *8*
wasps, eating 22
water, recycling urine into 16
Watkins, Perry (U.K.) 8
weddings
  balancing on bamboo poles 27
  child married to dog 22
  dog as best man 21
  dress bought on eBay 24

INDEX

weddings (*cont.*)
  dressed as *Shrek* characters 18
  multiple 21, 24
  in restaurant 27
  toasters as gifts 21
  twins marry twins 18
weights, lifting humans 21
Weisser, Elmar (Ger) 7
whale, saves free diver 25, *25*
wig, stops bullet 7
Woodward, Jack (U.K.) 21
worms, in lollipops 15
Wright brothers 9
writing, with feet 13
Wu Zhongyuan (Chn) 9

X
Xie Long (Chn) 18

Y
Yang Yun (Chn) 25, *25*

Z
Zhao Liang (Chn) 7
Zhou Haijue (Chn) 31
Zhou Juchang (Chn) 32
zip code, mail boat has own 8
zombie, job as 33
zoo, free admission for beards 7

ACKNOWLEDGMENTS

COVER (t) Sculptures from recycled steel by RoboSteel www.Robosteel.com, (c) Top Photo Group/Rex Features, (b) Jeff Barnett-Winsby; 6 (t, b) Guinness Rishi, (sp) © Rawlex—Fotolia.com; 8 Jeff Barnett-Winsby; 9 (t) Courtesy of NASA-JSC, (b) Khalid Tanveer/AP/Press Association Images; 10 East News/Rex Features; 11 © EuroPics[CEN]; 12–13 Wenn.com; 14 (t/l) AP/Press Association Images, (b) www.tropix.co.uk/V. and M. Birley; 15 Tony McNicol/Rex Features; 16 Reuters/Thomas Mukoya; 17 Wenn.com; 18 Wenn.com; 19 (b) © UPPA/Photoshot, (t) Wenn.com; 20 Rex Features; 21 David Lovere/Rex Features; 22 Kevin Walsh; 23 (c, b) Irish Revenue Commissioners, (t) David McLain /Getty Images; 24–25 © EuroPics[CEN]; 26–27 Tattoo by Dan Hazelton; 28 (t) Wenn.com, (c) Reuters/Nozim Kalandarov, (b) Reuters/Nir Elias; 29 (t) Wenn.com, (l) Top Photo Group/Rex Features, (r) Reuters/Adrees Latif; 30 AP/Press Association Images; 31 © EuroPics[CEN]; 32–33 Sculptures from recycled steel by RoboSteel www.Robosteel.com; BACK COVER Courtesy of NASA-JSC

Key: t = top, b = bottom, c = center, l = left, r = right, sp = single page, dp = double page

All other photos are from Ripley Entertainment Inc.
Every attempt has been made to acknowledge correctly and contact copyright holders and we apologize in advance for any unintentional errors or omissions, which will be corrected in future editions.